70

Lance W. Reedinger

Red Moon Press— Baltimore, MD
ISBN: 978-0578288406
Library of Congress Control Number: 2022906749
Title: *70*
Author: Lance W. Reedinger
Digital distribution | 2022
Paperback | 2022

Dedication

For Anne Rice

Thank you for those beautiful nightmares.

Chapter One
OCTOBER 1ˢᵗ

Abounding ball had eyes for the outfield until the quick Hispanic second baseman darted to his right and barehandedly grasp the leather sphere. A quick pirouette and the strong stout athlete fired a perfect laser to his eager teammate at first base. The ball popped the mitt a second before the thump of cleats pounded against the square white rubber. Collective moaning rattled from the crowd, through the television speakers, seeping into Robert's ears. The damn Yankees found a way to win again he mumbled to himself. Disgusted with the result, the old man closed his eyes and methodically tilted his head back against the sofa. Searing heat surged through his chest causing him to quickly jerk forward. Equal parts a steady diet of microwaved meals coupled with the dismay over the bums blowing another three-run lead caused the inflammation. Robert exhaled hard then grimaced as he tried to fight through the flare. The steady thump of his heart slowed down as the heat subsided in his chest. Clumsily, Robert reached for his cool soda on the table in front of him and knocked the glass over. Brown liquid poured over the simple wooden top, spilling with ease onto the grey carpet below. Leaning back once more in disgust, the last six months came crashing down like an avalanche of bad news from a dark press. All remaining light exited the room as the smart television went blank from its predetermined settings. Breathing steadily now, Robert, Bob to everyone in the known world, closed his eyes and finally broke. He wore the mask of a brave face the last six months. That mask was quickly replaced by a sobbing frightened creature mired in the depths of depression. A steady dripping sound, from the overturned drink hitting the carpet, started the melody. The subconscious somber tune played through his temple. The first track was how had it come to this.

Her vision appeared first, smiling back at him from the sliding glass door she had gone through thousands of times for an end of the day night smoke. Wavy dirty blonde straw hair without a hint of grey swirled around her as she stepped outside, leaving the slider open to let in the first refreshing blast of spring air. Robert's Seventieth birthday had been hectic as most of his life had been. Two days of preparations, last minute invitations, concluding with the inevitable clean up afterwards. As his love exhaled a puff outside, Robert thought he had finally found peace. Fully prepared for the golden years of relaxation. The only son of a hospital administrator and stay at home mother, he was pre-determined to work in the medical field. Relentlessly achieving in athletics as well as the class room. At age twenty-three, Robert Robinson received his nursing pin along with leading his collegiate baseball team in shutouts. Sprinting through little league and elementary school to division two baseball and college, Robert was ready to work hard and play hard, but his first shift at the hospital changed all of that. There she was signing out as he was signing in for the night shift. A high school sweetheart along with some liaisons at University, the eternally over achieving young man never had the desire nor time to fall in love. Mary O'Neil changed all of that with a freckled face smile and emerald eyes that pierced his heart. Robert Robinson courted her over several months as she finished her nursing residency, gathering a pin of her own. Destiny attached the two lovers at the hip, and they never separated. Spending their twenties living the upper middle-class dream. Traveling up and down the coast, three time a week restaurant outings, and summers on their boat came to halt when Mary whispered she was with child on a hot August night. His eternal love shared the joyous news on the same simple deck where she met her end. Matthew Robinson shared the exact day of his father's birth and the exact day and hour as his mother's death. April first, a cosmic joke dealt from the stars to the Robinson family. Mary and Robert were lovingly enchanted with their brown-haired boy. The couple decided Matthew was so perfect they dare not test fate by having another. Matthew, like his father, achieved on the athletic field and in all his scholastic endeavors. Matthew's sport was lacrosse instead of baseball, his pre-determined course of study was doctorate from the jump because that is progression in America. It all happened so fast. Never a regret. Never a moment to breath. Robert's existence was a nonstop express train of achievements and happiness until she fell.

Inhaling deeply then exhaling slowly, the swell of sullen tears began to pour from his eyelids like a waterfall of wallowing misery. Slowly leaning horizontally, Robert rested his head on the uncomfortable couch pillow. The old man began desperately praying for sleep. Another warm surge crept into his chest from the changing of positions, exacerbated by the incoming flashback of his love's demise. Closing his eyes once again, the last six months exploded thru his temple like a fright flight headed for a doomed destination. The thud of her fall rang a thunderous echo in Robert's head. At first, he nervously giggled, thinking the extra glass of merlot caused her to tumble. Walking slowly over to the love of his life, the reason for his being, sweat brought on by fear, broke out over his aged body. Forty-Seven years in medicine and Robert knew she was stone cold dead as he cowered next to her already cooling corpse. An hour later, the paramedics carried his heart out of their home like a meat sack covered in a black leather death shroud. Once again, duty took precedence over emotion. Making that call to Matthew, arranging the service, preparing the house for mourners. Robert never had time in life to rest, he had no time in death to mourn as well. A six-month tornado swept through his life trouncing all hopes and desires that he and Mary had of their new life of restful bliss. Matthew, encouraged by his horrid wife, convinced a somber father to sell off the house and move to the new modest senior community to relieve stress. More than likely, it was to make sure the tremendous equity put in the house would be secured. It all seemed like a good idea at the time. No yard work, no repairs, no ghost to float around familiar furniture where they had shared a lifetime of joyous memories. Planned long weekends up north and winters down south, quiet evenings spent with him watching ball games and her darting through mystery novels were all erased by an undetected embolism. Dreams of their golden years were replaced by ready-made meals with sulking solitude served as dessert. Shortly after Mary was laid to rest, condolences and visits went from frequent to non-existent. Robert quickly came to realize that his friends, were their friends. That couples' nights out were awkward when one flew solo. That a lifetime of hard work and family obligations left little room for lifelong relationships. Most of his softball buddies had died off or moved south along with his colleagues in the medical field. His dedication to work and economically conservative lifestyle left

Robert with a very nice monthly retirement check. To the delight of his daughter in law, also assured that he would not need to touch his savings nor the equity from the house, but it did nothing to compensate for love, companionship, or reason to exist in a world seemingly left behind. More morbid images flooded through Robert's temple before he slipped into deep sleep. The Shores at Sparrows Point seemed the logical choice. Not the monthly multi-thousand-dollar retirement communities that ripped life savings from seniors like a carnivorous clawed eagle, nor a rundown dungeon facility that was a mold ridden waiting room for the afterlife. The Shores offered simple and affordable senior apartment living. A nice place for a great price. Robert painted a smile on his pallet on move in day for his son and grandkids to show strength and assurance, but the sight of his new neighbors exacerbated the oncoming of massive depression. Playing softball well into his fifties and long nights at the hospital on his feet kept Robert in decent shape. Gifting him the appearance of looking ten years younger than his true age. The residents at The Shores moved like wounded sheep wandering towards death sheers, assisted to their end with metal walkers. The daily sight of his neighbors became a consistent reminder that any night could be his last. At times, a welcomed relief to the loneliness that plagued his current existence. Fluorescent lighting illuminated the five-story building throughout, seemingly sucking the last life force of its inhabitants. Matthew had the new furniture along with all his father's belongings set up to ease the shock from going from a classic Victorian to a standard two-bedroom apartment. Three months in, as he lay sobbing to sleep, his new home only felt like a twelve hundred square foot coffin, with microwave included. One final thought sprinted through his frightening flashback before mental exhaustion took over and carried the weeping figure to a solemn slumber. What the hell good did it do to be a good man in such a cruel world.

Chapter Two
October 2nd

A sharp pain shot through Robert's neck as he exited the car, making way toward the entrance of the mall. An hour earlier the weary old man wiped dried tears from his cheeks as he woke in a horrifically awkward position on the sofa after dozing off in an ocean of self-pity. Soaking in the warm shower helped wash away the depressing flashback episode from the night. Walking and window shopping at the local mall was an old pastime. Robert believed the brisk exercise and sounds of a crowd would help to ease his loneliness. Cool fall air greeted him as he stepped away from his car and headed toward the giant arc shaped glass doors that welcomed the public to part with their hard-earned money. Shaking his head slowly left to right, he got the creek out of his neck, fully ready to flush away the misery and get back to some semblance of a happier existence. The commercial excursion started well enough with the sweet warm smells of the food court meeting him at the circular entrance. Stealing a quick glance over to the Pretzel Palace, Robert decided warm salted bread with cool cheese partnered with a nice large ice filled soda would be his reward for making it through the vast labyrinth of corporate commerce. Already feeling better, the first of several events sent him spiraling back into a redundant depression. Being a creature of habit, Robert took the first step on the escalator as it ascended to the top flight of the three-story mall. Always going top to bottom was his eternal navigation system for mall walking. A young mother and child glided down the opposite flight of automated steps. Their descent triggered his angst at this new, scary, unfamiliar world. As the young child of no more than three went to her hands and knees, seemingly wanting to be swallowed by the gaps in the dangerous mechanically motioned steps, Robert nearly gasped noticing the mother's eyes were stapled to her phone. Never one to interfere in other's affairs, Robert let out a loud cough in desperate attempt to distract the mother from her phone and perhaps draw attention to her daughter's deadly dive toward certain doom. His cough did nothing to interrupt a loud media video that surely must have been sent from the lord himself, giving fair excuse for her complete ignorance to the well-being of her child. Robert closed his eyes, let out a deep sigh, and completed his free ride to the pinnacle of the building. Trying to remove the image of the child being swallowed by the metallic monster, the old man took the third floor by storm at a brisk pace without incident. Reaching the standard staircase, he gingerly grasped the railing before starting a slow walk down the steps. His creaking knees needed the assistance of the metal rails as most old ballplayers do. ROYS, a large clothing department store, welcomed Robert as he reached the second story. Some new sweaters for the fall season seemed to be a good idea. Quickly bypassing the female portion of the store, Robert entered a maze of perfectly hung male attire that begged for his attention. After sifting through the cavalcade of exotic-colored tops he found some more basic one toned heavy pullovers that fit his simplistic style. Robert removed a heavy grey turtleneck that looked perfect for the brisk cool nights ahead. The conservative man nearly chocked glancing at the price tag. Seventy-five dollars for cotton with a bear symbol clumsily sewn on the left breast sent him into a state of economic disbelief. Spending a life in medical scrubs and athletic gear, it was always Mary that had purchased all his proper clothes. The thought of her almost sent another wave from the sulking sea over him if not for the voice that crept up like doom on a broomstick.

"The Bear brand is one of our most popular collections for sophisticated men like yourself," the saleswoman spoke, entirely too loudly to be respected.

Robert turned and was greeted by a pudgy middle-aged woman adorning an employee tag that read Helen.

"Oh yeah, boy I tell ya, for this price it should come with pants and shoes," Robert replied, trying on one of his old dad jokes.

Helen's bubbly demeanor disappeared as she quickly realized her sale was out the window, she responded.

"My dad is on a budget as well, he shops at the thrift store down the street, they have good stuff for elderly people on a budget."

Robert began a response but was taken back as Helen turned quickly from him, waddling her way toward her next victim. He was desperate to chase after her, tell her that his decades of medical service provided him with savings that she could never hope to achieve, that he could well enough purchase the entire rack of smiling bear sweaters without blinking an eye, that a woman of her age, at that weight, would be having vascular surgery in the near future. Instead, he neatly placed the top back where he found it and made for a quick exit from Helen and her gaudy cotton kingdom. Hunger groans rumbled from his stomach, helping to cool his rising temper. The thought of the warm pretzel helped to get inattentive mother and ignorant Helen out of Robert's cloudy thoughts. A young man stood before him at Pretzel Palace, contemplating an order with the intensity of selecting a new automobile. The complexity of the order had Robert beginning to wonder if he had died in his sleep and awoken on another planet. Five combo orders were clearly placed above the small stand for convenience of both patron and employee, but this man was preparing an order only fit for a five-star restaurant. Mix the sour cream with the cheese, one half salted, and one half not salted pretzel, soft drink with only a few ice cubes. Each delusional demand heated Robert's chest. Annoyance turned to fury at the sight before him as the young man felt the need to instruct the pretzel lady on exactly how to mix his fixings. Once again, Robert held his nerve and waited patiently for the demanding debacle to conclude. Several minutes later, he parked at one of the metal chairs that sat next to a simple dining table and had to start laughing to keep from crying. The cheese and breaded crust alleviated the anxiety from the public horror that had played out in sorrowing slow motion. Quickly finishing with his much-needed snack, an encore was about to take place. Just to his left, a young couple were inhaling each other in a kiss fit for a steamy midnight movie. Mary and he had stolen many public kisses in their youth, but this was well beyond a quick peck of affection. Before turning away from the scene, Robert noticed the young woman's hand was under the cheap food court table motioning back and forth. Praying that guy still had his pecker in his pants, Robert slowly got up, disposed of his grease covered wrappings and was happy to exit the mall, the parking lot, and perhaps the entire known world.

Grey clouds covered the autumn sky, giving the appearance of evening instead of mid-day as Robert pulled his car into the lot of the Shores. One PM shot back from the car radio clock; he was hoping it was much later. Much later meant less time to ponder the circumstances of his mental demise. Much later meant preparing for his senior job at the store tomorrow. Much later meant a return to routine and routine was quickly becoming ever so important to block out the current state of affairs. The trip to the mall was supposed to shake the fear induced anxiety that built slowly over the last six months, erupting quickly last night. However, the quick trip only intensified those emotions as he passed through the automated glass doors and into the lobby of The Shores. Pumpkin spiced air freshener and Vaseline were the scents that exploded all through the entrance of the facility. Feeling the last six months coming to a head and the last fourteen hours trigger a beginning to the end, Robert began to accept his fate and completely lose his will to go on until an old angel called his name.

"Bobaroo!" she yelped, her voice echoing off of the cheap drywall that encompassed the lobby.

Forty-seven years working with hundreds of female nurses, Robert instantly recognized the sweet sound of Katie Voller. From the day he first saw Mary until this very moment, never once had he had an inkling of infidelity; however, being a red-blooded American male, on occasion a passing thought would arise along with quick glances at beautiful woman. None of those beauties had ever compared to the vision of Katie. Barely five-foot tall, long golden curly hair, angelic face, and it could not go without notice, insanely large breast which should have been disproportionate on her slim frame but sat stacked like the perfect final stroke to a flesh painted masterpiece. Even her bunny style front two teeth appeared perfectly placed by the almighty himself, adding to her intoxicating allure. Not satisfied with physical perfection, Katie was also one of the most dedicated and endearing co-workers Robert had ever known. Sweet as a Georgia peach, her positive bubbly personality was infections. Before his mental playbook recollection concluded, Katie had her arms around him. Her perfume dissipating the stench of the last six months, bringing forth a feeling he had not had during that period. Hope.

"Jesus Katie, what are you doing here?" Robert questioned, fumbling for his words due to the shock of her unexpected presence.

"Was just passing through on my way south and wanted to check on ya, which way to your digs buddy?" Katie replied, sensing her arrival was more shocking to the widower than she had expected, as well as feeling the ever-present weight of the old eyes in the lobby examining the younger gorgeous woman with the much older man.

Still smiling, Robert pointed toward the right hallway leading to his apartment. Katie retrieved two black paper bags from the foot of the waiting chair she had been seated in for around an hour, waiting on her old friend's arrival. The two former colleagues started down the long hallway, step in step over the cheap faux grey wooden laminate floor. Passing each apartment door with their built-out shelves filled with the cherubic faces of grandchildren.

"I'm so sorry about Mary, Bob, how you holding up big guy?" Katie questioned, with a reassuring arm pat to his shoulder.

"Good, really good, hey, spending forty-seven years with the love of your life is blessing," Robert replied. He retrieved his key card with a slight tremble in his hand. Lying was not his forte.

A little light went from red to green on the digital lock. Robert welcomed his former favorite nurse into his living coffin. Katie followed behind him, immediately prancing into the kitchen, popping open the cherry cabinets in search for glasses. Smiling at her welcomed intrusion, Robert headed into the living room, took off his wind jacket, and plumped down on the corner of the sofa. Same spot he awoke from in an entirely different spirit hours ago.

"Any wine glasses Bobaroo?" Katie asked, noticing that none of the glassware looked used as they sat in perfect position, probably from the day they were first put there.

"Nah, sorry, haven't had a chance to pick up anything formal yet. Just a half glass for me, it's a school night," Robert replied.

"School night? Man, are you still working?" Katie inquired, now pouring a thick dark red into one of the standard sized glasses.

"Yeah, got a job at Dollar Land, keeps me moving."

Katie turned the corner and entered the living area with two three quarters filled glasses, both stained in a thick dark crimson. She handed Robert one glass and placed her drink on the end table then took off her tight leather jacket, revealing a low-cut short sleeve shirt that barely contained her massive breasts. Robert quickly put his drink to his lips to avert his eyes from the devil's candy. The drink was thick, rich, and had a slight taste of copper to it. The small sip helped avert his sinister stare but only enhanced the unfamiliar rise in his jogging pants. He took a brief moment to compose himself before meeting Katie's sparkling blue eyes to catch up.

"How did you find me?" Robert questioned, with a big smile, exposing his white teeth, now tainted a shade of red.

"It's twenty-twenty-two Bobaroo, you can find anyone with three clicks on a phone. The real question is how are you really doing, because with all love, you really look like shit," Katie responded, with an inquisitive smile.

"Well, it's been an adjustment, that's for sure. But slowly I'm finding my way around this new existence," Robert responded, lying again as not wanting to ruin a happy reunion.

"Nothing wrong with letting it out Bobaroo. I've never been in love. I don't have any answers or great wisdom to pass along, but as long as you're here, all I can say is keep trucking," Katie preached, raising her glass to his as they toasted.

"Well, I may look like shit, but damn missy you haven't aged a day. What's it been about ten years?"

"Yeah, around about that. Life of a traveling nurse, keeps ya young," Katie replied, with a slightly more forced smile. Lying was not her forte either.

"And no prick doctor has snatched you up yet? What the hell you waiting for? As you can see, life has a way of accelerating quickly. I know you've had your fun, when are you going to grow roots and sprout fruits?" Robert prodded, taking another, longer swig from the uniquely tasting wine.

Katie giggled at Robert's bluntness. But that was always him, respectful but brutally honest. A trait lost on the modern male. The two replayed their history. Katie's first night under his department. All the looks of the male patients as she would enter their rooms. Her very essence peaking the sickest souls' spirits. One glass became one bottle. After a few hours the last drop of the second bottle filled the rims of their glasses. Feeling a little buzzed but not off his ass drunk, Robert chalked it up to the joy of his company keeping him from fall down drunk mode. With the first sip of the last glass, Robert began to ask Katie what hospital she was heading to when he noticed her approaching him slowly. He recoiled from an unfamiliar face. Katie's round angelic mask seemed tighter and daunting. Those famous crystal blue eyes narrowing and shading darker as she appeared to slither across the sofa toward him. Her small soft hands that caressed patients on their death bed, now curled into animal like paws. Katie smiled as she reached Robert, those bunny teeth incisors appearing to be dwarfed by two growing canines. Robert's eyes began to gloss over as the most serine feeling encompassed his entire body. The next few moments were a strobe light snapshot blinking through his temple. Katie walking him to his bed, whispering something about read the letter, followed by complete darkness. Not the darkness that accompanies a deep sleep, total darkness. An abyss of darkness poured through him as his mystical rebirth began.

Chapter Three
October 3rd

Tropical melodies sounded in the distant as old eyes peeled open to greet the day. Robert inhaled deeply then reached for the source of the tune, swiping right on his phone to disarm the harmonic alarm. Accustomed to shaking the cobwebs out to clearly see the front of his cellular, he was a tad startled to see seven AM look back at him clear as the Caribbean sea. Another deep breath and with the vigor of a younger man Robert nearly catapulted out of bed, quickly making way to the bathroom. After a quick piss he began to undress for a warm shower. Sitting on the toilet another oddity broke up the robotic routine. Prepared to remove his socks, the sneakers from yesterday's excursion were still tightly laced to his feet. The previous night's encounter came flushing back into memory. Slowly stripping from shoe to shirt, Robert tried to recall the last moment of the evening in hope of explaining how he had ended up in bed fully clothed and sneaker strapped. Katie explaining where she was headed next for work, Robert lecturing on the archaic system of hospitals in the south, then Katie seemingly locking eyes with her old mentor as she seductively approached him. Fully undressed, he tilted his head back and moaned. Not having more than a beer or two since Mary passed, a silent prayer was sent to the heavens, hoping the excessive intake of the unique wine did not lead to any sort of inappropriate behavior. Turning toward the lowered sink, built for seniors but causing him to awkwardly lurch every time to turn the faucet, a mental note was made to contact Katie right after work. Cold water gushed from the faucet and an unfamiliar vision peered back from the mirror. Robert's roundish face looked more defined. The old man's cheek bones perfectly protruded to the side of his mouth. A white, tight, crew cut hairstyle had turned to a full-on salt and pepper appearance, more pepper than salt. The few brown circles that had sprung around an aged temple seemingly stole off into the night. Glancing down, collarbones descended towards a tight torso and a four pack that the very active man had maintained well into his fifties. Once more peering into the mirror for a closer examination. Robert searched for the lines that dug in around his eyes and cut deep into his forehead. An aged but fresh-faced reflection stared back at him. His routine internal clock kicked in as he took his toothbrush from its metallic holder, applied the baking soda brand paste, and started brushing furiously. Brushing and spitting, the odd transformation was chalked up to a nice visit from an old friend mixed with the antioxidant healing power of red wine. Seeing the effects of positivity and limited alcohol for decades in the field, Robert quickly dismissed the miraculous metamorphosis as thoughts fluttered back to Katie. Expecting a day-old stubble, there was no need for the razor today as no miniscule hairs had rose on this new younger man's flesh mask. Robert closed the medicine cabinet and cranked on the shower. A warm October morning caused heat to sneak in through the bathroom window, sneaking in through the wooded slates, but Robert still felt chilly and turned the hot knob on full blast while keeping the cold knob at a quarter turn. Letting the hot water explode over his back, he leaned forward in attempt to fight off a chill. Hoping this was no onset to a cold, the chilly figure turned, attempting to get warmer by soaking his head under the cascade of heated water. Several minutes later feeling fresh as a daisy, Robert pulled on his cotton polo yellow uniform and made for work. Mary smiled back at him from the photo on his bedstand as he rubbed his thumb down the side of the silver frame. Cooling heat torched his thumb, the kind you get when touching dry ice, causing him to quickly withdraw his hand. The skin on the thumb went rock hard as if barely touching a heated electric top stove, then instantly appeared to heal before going soft again. Wanting to stop for a quick bite before work, Robert dismissed the physical oddity as he bounded for the door. The large manilla envelope on the living room table with his name and the words, read as soon as you get up, written in very large letters, was ignored.

Soft rain pelted the roof of the sub compact car as Robert sat in the strip mall parking lot ready to consume a quick breakfast before his shift. The hash brown he wolfed down on the drive over was bland beyond belief. The orange juice he sipped at each red light tasted more like tap water than the desired refreshing pick me up he had hoped for. Unwrapping the sausage and egg sandwich brought on hope of something more filling, but the first bite proved to be another disappointment. Perhaps the over consumption of the wine last night numbed his tastebuds, Robert thought, as he pondered whether a Gatorade and Tylenol would have been a better option to start the day. Still ten minutes until open and not seeing any of his co-workers parked yet, the old man glanced through the drizzle-soaked front window, silently observing as employees and patrons moved like cattle in and out of the stores that made up the shopping center. All of them in a hurry to go nowhere quickly. As a pop star sang of another broken relationship from the radio Robert turned and saw a mother and two of her small children exit an overpriced SUV and headed right past him toward the shops. Giving a quick head nod as not to give the appearance of staring at the vulnerable trio, his eyes awkwardly became fixed to one the young child's soft neck. Blue lines appeared to bulge from under the boy's skin, the blood beneath called out to be released. Their mother missed the head nod and gave a nasty scowl at the weird old man as she quickly hurried her babies past his rain-soaked car. A loud beep interrupted the stare down. Dawn waived from her old pickup.

"Let's get at it young man," Dawn barked, as she and Debbie descended out of their truck, briskly walking past Robert.

Dawn and Debbie had managed Dollar Land since Central Park was a plant. A month ago, the department of aging had a job fair for seniors at the Shores. Robert thought a part time job would be great to steady his mental sinking ship. Mary knew the two women who shared a career in retail as well as an apartment together. She would return from the thrift store with cheap paperbacks, snacks, and tales of the two funny foul-mouthed ladies. Pleased to see Dollar Land needing a part time stocker, Robert went to the interview and the duo hired him on the spot. A couple days a week to stock shelves and spot clean was a much needed physical and mental workout. Not needing the money, Robert was still shocked at the wage offered. Never looking down at those who did not take their education or careers seriously, he pondered every shift at the store, how can anyone live off this? Dawn turned the key to the automatic doors and the three entered the seventy-five hundred square foot store. During his first week, Robert quickly learned that the time for small talk was to take place once the opening chores were complete. Dawn took to the job as a titan of industry rather than a simple manager of a discounted retailer. Debbie, her assistant in name only, was much more laid back. Robert headed for the utility closet to prep the morning mop as Dawn barked about Bruce being late again. Bruce was the only other full-time employee, head stocker, and key holder. Robert did not know any of the other team of part-timers as Dawn had them on afternoon and closing shifts. Dipshits can't get up on time she would remind everyone daily. Chemical scents exploded into his nostrils after opening the utility door. Lemon scented floor cleaner was poured into the yellow bucket accompanying the dirty water that came from the store's cleaning sink. Moments later, it was down aisle one giving the back and forth a go while shoe stains disappeared beneath the lemon scented strings doused with soapy water. The usually heavy wooden handle felt like a feather today. Looking younger, feeling stronger, Robert flew through the aisles with ease and with an actual, not forced, smile adorning his face. Back in the utility closet, he could hear Dawn laying into Bruce again, the weekly tirade for tardiness, staring at his phone too long and mislabeling. Dawn was tough as a coffin nail but had a heart of gold. It was known that in thirty years, she had never fired an employee except for theft, which she explained to Robert during his interview, was like stealing from her pocketbook. Robert met Bruce back in the stock room, ready to roll out the U-boats of cheap goods filled with stale snacks.

"Can't believe they blew that lead again," Bruce said, grabbing the first loaded cart.

"Damn, again! I missed it last night, had some company over," Robert replied.

"Company huh? You wrangling in those snow birds buddy?"

"My time with that has come and gone young buck."

"It's never too late to get back on the mound buddy."

They laughed some more and got back to their daily task. Baseball was the only thing the two had in common. Robert was thankful for that. Bruce was a free-spirited homosexual, tech obsessed, undisciplined young man. Everything Robert was not, at first, he feared the two would collide like oil and vinegar. Quickly, Robert came to really enjoy the young man's company. Bruce moved and lived at a pace Robert quickly recognized as severe ADD disorder. The older, experienced man wanted to help Bruce move on from his two years at Dollar Land and fourth year at community college. He wanted to help Bruce get direction, teach him economic discipline, get the courage to leave his abusive lover, but in the end, Robert just enjoyed talking with the young man about baseball, movies, and freaks that frequented the store daily. Bruce treated the old man with complete respect and kindness. Robert hoped this was the nature of the young adult, not the fact that he would usually get hit up for a twenty here and there. Bruce always offered to pay the loans back, but Robert always told the thin youngster to put it on his tab. Around forty bucks a week was a small fee for some welcomed companionship and Bruce's mentoring the out of touch senior on the new ways of the world. Very grateful for Bruce's lectures on what vocabulary is used and not used in order to refrain from being offensive in the modern world. Drizzle turned to a steady downpour as the two leisurely refilled home goods, canned foods, and paper products. Robert putting the young man to shame with his speed and efficiency while Bruce spent most of his time glaring at his phone laughing. The bad weather meant few patrons today. Dawn was parked in the office doing paperwork while Debbie stood bored at the front counter reading tabloid magazines.

"Stepping out for a smoke bud," Bruce yelped, eyes still glued to his phone.

The lazy kid always made a habit of taking a smoke when it came time to stock the heavy detergents. With no hint of any even average muscle mass, Bruce could not weigh more than a buck fifty Robert calculated. Usually waiting for his co-worker to finish his calculated smoke, Robert felt good today, so he pushed the awkward carrier to the back of the store. As Bruce passed him, Robert noticed under the unnecessary foundation Bruce caked on his young face, a purple-colored bruise under his eye. No stranger to domestic cases at the hospital, Robert let out a disgusted moan. Reaching the destination for the detergents and bleach, he quickly popped open the tough cardboard with ease. There was a time when he could throw the pill at ninety plus, but these days it was tough labor tossing heavy liquids. A new found strength took over as he began tossing the heavy containers like they were a toddler's rattle in a giant's hand.

"Hi, can you tell me where they moved the makeup to?" A young woman questioned behind him.

Before responding, Robert shook his head and pondered. The store literally had twelve aisles, was this generation so lazy they could not make the short trip around the store to locate items. After an annoyed exhale, he turned around and viewed a pretty young woman of no more than thirty. She wore pajama pants and a sweatshirt with some musician's face printed on it.

"Second aisle, near the front of the store," Robert instructed, with a forced smile.

"Oh cool, hey do you work here a lot. I usually come in at night but was up early today," the young woman questioned, her cheeks turning a shade of red.

"Ah, a couple of mornings here and there. It's good to keep active at my age."

"I like older guys. We should hang sometime. The pub at the end of the block has dollar drafts tonight," the woman said, opening her mouth and licking the top of her teeth after finishing her offer.

Robert gave a little laugh and replied, "I'm married but I'm sure lots of young men would like to throw a few back with you."

"Lucky girl, well I'll see ya around hottie," the woman said, as she turned and headed toward the cheap makeup.

Robert stared at the back of her neck in wonder as she walked away. Bruce had lectured him about the girls in the neighborhood looking for sugar daddies, but this was his first experience. He kind of liked it and for the second time in twenty-four hours, felt a rise down below.

After the six-hour shift concluded, Robert parked his car at The Shores feeling the best he had since Mary left this world. Contacting Katie was his first priority once he got settled. A desperate feeling to need to apologize sprang new anxieties. Exacerbated by desperately wanting to piece together the finale of their encounter last night. After that, a trip to the pub tonight seemed like a good idea. No need to sulk any longer, no need to waist whatever days he had left, no need to wallow, she was not coming back. With renewed vigor, Robert exited his car and walked slowly toward the building entrance. Rays of sunlight had finally broken through the overcast clouds. The bright beams seemed to seep his energy and renewed positive energy. Robert glared up at the late afternoon sun then immediately shut his eyes. The heated radiation appeared to shine down on him with fury and rage. Glaring toward the pavement below with shielded eyes now pointed downward, a voice shouted repetitive curses from the corner of the parking lot.

"Oh Shit! Oh Shit! Oh Shit!" the familiar voice squeaked.
Robert did not have to search for Katie. She found him. Again.

Chapter Four
October 4th

Large green neon lights blinked from the overhead microwave alerting Robert that midnight had come, birthing the day October fourth, twenty-twenty two. His trance was broken by the flashing signal as he gazed back down to the small dead mouse encompassed in aluminum foil. Midnight meant Robert had been staring over his cut-out dining room into the darkness of the living area for well over an hour since Katie departed. The inexplicable news dealt to him over the course of the last several hours induced the trance. Desperately needing to lay down, Robert quickly crumbled the foil over the exposed portions of the mouse and deposited the rodent in the bin. Striding over to the sink to remove any bacteria, he turned the faucet on, warm water flowed from the adjustable sprout. Robert flicked the handle upward and gazed out from the kitchen once more, realizing he need not worry about bacteria ever again. Boy, was there so much more to worry about now though. A loud bump from his new pet flinging itself against its glass prison interrupted another standing comatose state. For the first time in ages the creature of habit ignored his pre sleep routine on purpose. Did he ever have to brush his teeth again? Wash his face and exfoliate again? Remove build up from his ear again? Katie gave many answers but there were still so many questions. Questions popped up all around him like a rapid-fire game show quiz without a host. Seventy-five was the temperature announced from the digital thermostat, but his skin was chilly and would remain so, as explained earlier. Still the pragmatist, Robert grabbed the heavy fleece blanket from the sofa instead of dialing up the heat. A thick bed quilt and fleece did the trick as he pulled them both tightly up to his neck. Robert closed his eyes, ready to reflect on what the hell had just happened. Hoping beyond hope that this was some disillusioned dream brought on by consistent depression as he had seen numerous times before during numerous consulting sessions at area psych wards. Another soft boom from his new buddy, not happy about its new home, assured him it was not. Robert shut his lids and replayed the evening's events.

After her curse filled fit, Katie stood motionless, just staring at her old friend with a covered large rectangle box in her hands.

"What's wrong girl?" Robert questioned.

"We have to get inside quick," Katie replied. The two old friends hurried quickly toward the apartment.

Always the gentlemen, Robert asked twice if he could help her with the large box. Katie slowly shook her head side to side as she darted quickly ahead of him, tearing through the lobby like a golden tipped torpedo eager to reach its target. After catching up to her at his front door, Robert held the badge next to the accepting digital lock. Katie nearly took his arm off while he lifted the handle to crack open the entrance.

"Hey, Hey, Hey, slow down there kid. What the hell is going on?" Robert exclaimed, as he slowly closed and locked the door behind her.

In what seemed a flash, Katie sat the box on the kitchen countertop with force. She forcefully wrapped her hands around both of Robert's biceps.

"Buddy, please listen to me. Take a comfy seat and relax. We really need to talk," Katie instructed.

Anxiety coursed through the old man as he removed his jacket and took up his favorite spot at the edge of the sofa. Robert crossed his legs and started an immediate twitch tap with his left foot. An old habit that would drive Mary crazy when she tried to have a serious conversation with her lover. Robert reached for the remote, turning on the television in hopes the images and noise that came from the screen would alleviate the tension swirling around the room.

"Turn that off please!" Katie shouted.

Now brimming with fear and anxiety, he clicked off the set and stood.

"Sit please," Katie said, as she rounded her friend adorning a large pocketbook on her left shoulder which must have been in the box. Katie placed the pocketbook on the simple wooden table. She sat uncomfortably close to Robert, forcing a smile before she began.

"Guess ya didn't see the big ass envelope right here today, did ya?" Katie asked mockingly, as she picked up and tossed down the manilla carrier. Robert just shook his head no.

Putting on a calmer demeanor, Katie faced her old friend and started.

"Bobaroo, what I am about to tell you is going to be shocking and scary. Please be as calm as possible and try to relax and listen."

Robert leaned back, closed his eyes, and nodded vertically. His only thought was that he had done something completely inappropriate during their last encounter. Reflecting later in the night, he wished that were the case.

"I am a vampire Bob," Katie stated.

Robert chuckled and began to reply until he saw the blank stoic expression on her face. Katie's mug told no lie. She continued.

"Here is the real kicker, now you are one as well."

His snickering came to a sudden halt, his expression quickly mimicked hers.

"Uggghhh, were to start. Ok from the beginning. Well, back when we first met, I told you like everyone else before my rebirth that I was raised by my grandma and that she died, and I really did not have any family. Well. That is mostly true. I never knew my father and my mother was a junkie, so my grandparents raised me. Pops passed when I was in high school, so it was just Grannie and me. I was a good girl through and through. School, sports, socially, I always strived to make them proud. Pops and Grannie were so sweet but stern, careful to not let me fall into the same traps my mother, their only child, did. Grannie died shortly after I finished nursing school. She was so proud Bob, you would have loved her. Like you, she would tease, always wanting me to marry a doctor. Of course, with tits like these, scooping up a doc was like catching carp in a barrel. Before settling down too quick I did want to have a bit of fun before I picked one. It was the nineties and raves were all the rage."

Robert's dazed concentration faltered for a moment as he shot Katie an inquisitive look. She explained.

"Raves are dance parties, mostly in abandoned buildings with shitty music and shitty drugs."

Robert nodded, still bedazzled at what he was hearing. Katie continued,

"There I was, a smart girl just having a night out with a few other nurses when the most gorgeously exotic looking man I had ever seen stole my eyes. His skin was almost translucent. His eyes appeared to burst from their sockets, exploding lightning blue. Curly raven colored hair bounced around his head, crying out for me to stroke. We danced for hours on end and then he asked me to his car. It was crowded, there were people everywhere, so I had no worries about being harmed and no man that looked that good could be too bad. We walked hand in hand past a few cars, he pulled me close to him, shined those brilliant blues into my heart and then I blacked out. When I woke up, he was lying next to me with a sharped tooth smile. His loving locks falling over his shoulders like a black wave seducing a surfer. His name was Marcel. The vampire that gave me the night life as I did you. Our saga is a long one. A delicate tale for another time. Marcel sits with the council now and I am free to start my own nest."

Stumbling for words Robert asked, "Wait, ok before I shit my pants, one thing, did no one come looking for you?"

"Hold all questions for a hot minute Bobaroo, we got a lot to get through in a short time. You must remember that I had no close friends. My high school girls gave way to college girls and all of us went our separate ways after graduation. I was hardly a month into my first assignment when this happened. One of the nurses filled a missing person report but they all thought I ran off with this stunning man," Katie answered, then started again.

"So, a nest consists of three vamps who essentially roam the land together until one is called to council. Which is another drawn out story for another time. We have to get to business because I've got some more not so hot news to tell ya."

"More bad news! Wait, just hold up. This is batshit crazy little girl. If this is some October prank..." Robert started. Before he could finish Katie shot her head forward, two fangs protruded from her mouth accompanied by a deep hissing sound. Robert recoiled, nearly doing a backflip over the edge of the sectional.

"Bob please, just listen. I beg you. I did this because I love you," Katie pleaded. Her deep voice sounding demonic instead of that high pitched sweetness Robert was accustomed to. Katie slid a cushion down to ease the tension. Robert slowly took up his former position, this time with his left hand clawed into the arm of the sofa.

Katie continued. "Vamps usually turn those who are down and out. Homeless, orphaned, endlessly caught in the drip of addiction. Marcel choose me out of lust, I choose you out of love. I returned to nursing and moved around with Marcel and another vampire for years. Nursing was an easy way to score blood. In nearly twenty years in the medical field, I never met a more kind hearted, hardworking, devoted man than you. I never judged men for the way they looked at me nor the jealous musk of women. But your scent was always pure, the purest I have ever smelled. Never would I have thought of turning you until I heard of Mary's passing. I always keep tabs on those I have met through the years. After finding out about Mary's death I needed to see how you were. After a long period of self-consultation, I had to see you for myself, see how you would adjust without her. I stalked you for a couple of weeks. I saw a man with no friends, no family tending to your emotions, and no will to continue. I just had to. I hope you forgive me one day and enjoy this great gift."

Robert, still clutching the sofa eased a bit as Katie's face and fangs retracted back to the beautiful young woman he once knew.

"Just, just, give me a second to take this in. Shit. I need a drink," Robert said, slowly rising, he headed to the fridge. Aware that Katie had vulture eyes on him in case he tried to bolt. Manners never left him as he asked her if she wanted a drink as well. Katie declined. Returning with a cold canned beer Robert cautiously sat down on the couch, popped the metal lid, and took a long swig.

"Watered down, isn't it?" Katie asked.

"Yeah, probably went stale, been in the fridge probably a month," Robert replied.

"Nope, it's how everything will taste now. There are a few tricks though."

Remembering his bland breakfast in the morning and the awkwardly tasting canned chili he wolfed down at the store, Robert put his head in his hand, he let out a deep moan as truth began to take form from this tall tale.

"Buddy, that is just one minor thing compared to all the great things in store for you, I promise," Katie said.

"Ok, so say this really happening, I mean for real for real. What the hell comes next?" Robert probed.

Katie swiped a little red liquid from the side of her eye, upset that her friend was upset, she wiped it between her thumb and pointer finger before beginning again.

"Usually, I stay with you for a year while we plan your death and plot our future. I guide you through your new life as we embark on a great eternal adventure together. But."

Closing his eyes and taking another swig despite the empty taste, Robert questioned. "But what?"

"Well two things. One, I must leave right after this conversation. I turned my first a while back. It has been a bit of a rough transition. I only got news of Mary's passing from your son's social media account a few months ago. I had to leave her. There was an incident. I thought she would be ok on her own for a few weeks. Apparently, there has been a bit of a problem, so I must scram up north to check things out before returning. Then the three of us can start this great new life together."

"What kind of problem?" Robert asked.

"To be honest, I think she killed someone. We communicate through social media business pages. That is the message I got this morning. Two, um yeah. I really needed permission before turning you and did not get that exact permission. Allegedly, vamps are only supposed to be turned under the mortal age of thirty. I was never really given an explanation why, but I kind of get the reason now," Katie answered.

Another long swig and another question from Robert. "And why might that be?"

"The transformation starts with the taking of another vampire's blood. Which is what you drank the other night. Just about an entire bottle of my blood. This is done several times as vampire blood consumes all the mortal molecular cells. There are anomalies here and there, but I am taking an educated guess that the older the person, the quicker it works. That was the reason for my shit fit when I saw you pull in tonight. Have you looked in the mirror? You look a hot Fifty Bob, not Seventy. Be glad we live in a self-absorbed world were people only take notice of physical changes when it's for the worse."

Katie slowly inched closer to Robert as not to frighten him again.

"Relax please buddy, I need to check something."

She gently took his right hand into her own, in a flash her thumbnail protracted as she sliced deep into the middle of Robert's palm.

Robert shot straight up screaming from his lying position. Breathing heavy, his head darted back and forth examining the pitch-black room for no reason. Taking a deep breath, he took a look at his clock, which read five AM. A nightmare, it had to be all a nightmare he reassured himself. With no work and basically nothing at all to do for the day, Robert contemplated just laying back down and letting the morning get away from him until he felt the tiny sting in his right hand. The sting that snapped him out of the dream. The dream that Katie was a creature of the night, slicing into the meaty part of his hand all the way to bone to invoke a reaction. He threw himself back down again as the replay of the reaction came storming back into his thoughts. His yelp, ten trimmed fingernails unexplainably shooting into two-inch death talons, the tear in his lower lip as fangs emerged from his upper cavity. Robert opened his eyes slowly as he licked his bottom lip, feeling the tiniest of scabs that had already healed the identical puncture wounds. It was no nightmare, it was real. Robert replayed the conversation over again for the tenth time until his clock now read ten AM, when he decided to get up and at least give the day a go. Walking into the kitchen, the scent of the dead mouse blanketed the room. Robert poured a glass of orange juice, out of habit, and returned to his favorite spot on the sofa. Small tears in the grey fabric welcomed his left hand where he dug for his life as Katie revealed her night face. Placing his drink on the coaster, Robert picked up his night life notes, and it all came flooding back again. Katie left this for him to reference as a sort of sinister syllabus before she returned.

VAMPIRE 101

-The Sun will not kill you directly but will drain you into a hibernation state. Stay out of direct sunlight as much as possible. No more than two hours max. Taking shade for twenty minutes will completely restore your energy. Sunblock is a bit of a remedy but not a cure.

-You are now allergic to silver. Touching it will burn and enough of it can make you comatose.

25

-Eat all the garlic you want. It has no effect.

-Deck your house out in crucifixes. It has no effect.

-You are kind of, sort of, still alive, so you will show a reflection in a mirror and through a digital lens.

-Rule of 5: You are now five times faster than the fastest human. You are now five times stronger than any human. You have five times the sexual allure of any human. You heal five times faster than any human, but a mortal wound can still kill you instantly.

-You are immune to all mortal disease and sickness. You will never physically age. Consumption of blood may bring forth a more youthful appearance and enhance your supernatural gifts.

-One rule of 20: You have twenty times the senses of any human. You will hear sound from absurd distances. You will be able to smell twenty times stronger than any human as well as feel all range of emotions from humans by their scent.

-You cannot fly.

-You will piss, shit, cry, and cum blood from this day forth. CONTROL YOUR EMOTIONS!

-In a few days you will no longer have a heartbeat nor be breathing. DO NOT GO TO ANY MEDICAL PROFESSIONAL UNDER ANY CIRCUMSTANCES.

-Eat as usual as to not arouse suspension. Food and drink will no longer have any taste. A dose of blood may bring forth some semblance of flavor. You only need blood to survive. One mouse a week will keep you on the level.

Robert glanced over his new rules and regulations from Katie's written orientation. She went over these in detail over and over, making sure it all sunk in. He cringed when she brought the box into the living room, revealing a yellow corn snake. He was to buy two mice per week. One for him, one for the snake. Surely the reptile was illegal to have in the complex, but no one had come to visit for months. Katie gave a quick demonstration on the easiest way to slit the mouse's neck for a quick sip. Pouring half of the creature's blood into his empty beer can. She laughed as Robert squirmed after taking a swig, then applauded as she saw his eyes expand at the delight of the nocturnal nectar. Before leaving, Katie explained how they would dine on wild animals. She explained that the blood of a fresh doe was better than any five-star meal in Paris. Robert closed his eyes and saw his old friend bid him a good night, promising to be back in a few weeks to start a new night life for them both. He felt excited, nervous, afraid, anxious, and for the first time since his love left, Robert felt alive. How odd he thought, opening his eyes again, it took being undead to feel alive again. His new found smile dissipated a bit as he re-read the last line of his outline.

-UNDER NO CIRCUMSTANCE. DO NOT TASTE ANY HUMAN BLOOD!

Chapter Five
October 5th

Old eyes examined Robert as he walked through the lobby of The Shores. Effects of his rebirth were becoming rapidly evident. A toned middle-aged man replaced the much thicker older man that had solemnly slumbered to and from his apartment without saying much to his fellow residents. Several of the old ladies' guard that spent much of their remaining days in the lobby, watching like senior sentinels, began to whisper and giggle to each other. Robert gave them a quick nod as he hurried past the electronic front door. An autumn sun, covered by clouds, still seemed to ignite his exposed facial flesh as he turned left and started his walk of the grounds. No pool, tennis court, or gym at the modest retirement community, but The Shores offered a nice scenic walking path that led to the rocky banks of the Patapsco river, which flowed calmly into the Chesapeake. Robert needed to get out of his apartment. The last twenty-four hours were spent going over and over and over this new mad life bitten into him. From denial to acceptance and back to denial, the new vampire nearly went mad replaying Katie's visit. He wanted to call her, but phone contact was apparently forbidden. Katie only hinted toward consequences of exposure, assuring him that all would be revealed upon her return. She begged him to just lay low, quit his job, and start to prepare for an exciting new life. Tall hickory trees appeared to engulf him as he strolled toward the pier ahead. It was good to leave the apartment, but the cool fall air and brisk walk was doing nothing to alleviate the consistent mulling that pounded his worried temple. His physical form presented a man that should be taking the walk at ease, but the nocturnal effects caused Robert to labor before he reached the pier. He made way to a wooden bench next to the community dog park. Sitting with eyes closed, Robert tried to steady his mind. Several serene minutes passed as anxiety slipped into restful bliss. Robert concluded to just make a schedule until Katie's expected return. What was done was done. Eyes open and plan formed, he rose slowly and began his journey back when the ear shattering barking began. A little brown dachshund yapped at the sight of the night creature. Its owner, a tall white-haired woman, tried to offer an apology. "He never acts like this sir, I'm so sorry."

"No problem, he's probably just excited to go to the park," Robert replied.

The woman offered a smile as she attempted to pull the hot dog shaped mutt toward the dog park. Rex, as she consistently repeated, was not budging. Rex continued to howl at Robert as though he were the devil himself, ready to attack his owner. With a final tug, the old woman nearly ripped Rex's head off as she turned him from the odd man and toward the maze of dog park equipment. Sensing the struggle, Robert quickly made way out of the dog's radar. A quick glance back and he saw Rex, unleashed, start to hurdle the metallic bars and swoop around the play area to the delight of his owner. Even from afar, the veins pulsing from the small dog's neck seemed to beckon a bite. Robert pondered if all animals would take to him like this. With a grimace he also pondered if he would always crave their meaty fur covered flesh. Yet another question for Katie, who left him like a pilot without wings. The dog and the sun had zapped much of the new vampire's energy. He moved quickly toward the shelter of the complex, desperate to get back inside when he remembered. The dog. Same as Sasha's dog. Sasha, his self-important, loathsome, arrogant daughter in law. The one he would be dining with tonight. It was the fifth and he had dinner plans at his son's house later in the evening.

"Hey Matty!" Robert shouted. As his grandson opened the large door.

"Hey Pop," Matty responded, barely glancing before walking away. Eyes fixed on his tablet.

Robert entered the foyer in search for his son and his son's heinous wife. A massive television blared to his right where Matty and Marco, his little brother, sat glued to their electronic devices. The shine from the massive chandelier above felt like it carried the heat of the sun as Robert put his hand over his eyes while glancing upwards to the second story indoor balcony.

"We're in here Bob!" Yelled a female voice from the kitchen area.

Robert made his way toward the back of the obnoxiously large brick mansion, careful to walk around the rugs that hugged the designer ceramic floor.

"Hey there little lady," Robert announced, as he arrived at the gargantuan kitchen with a smile plastered on his paler than usual face. Knowing that little lady was a term she did not take to.

Sasha seemed to ignore the small dig as she furiously mixed the leafy ingredients inside the large salad bowl.

"There's beer in the fridge, we are dining in here tonight. I'm redoing the formal dining area this month," Sasha explained, while she continued to obsessively toss perfectly chopped celery pieces into a large wooden bowl.

Robert nodded as he headed toward the tall stainless-steel fridge that had more gadgets than his car. The door flew open as Matthew entered ass first, his large hands grasping a silver looking tray filled with meaty steaks. In his mortal life, Robert would have salivated at the sight of the meat, but he just remembered, those things are going to taste like paper and that tray looked dangerous. Another glancing thought passed, he had not eaten in nearly two days, yet had not the hint of hunger. Katie said one mouse a week would be filling, she also gave him a shot of her own blood to tide him over, explaining he would only need one trip to the pet store before her return.

"Hey Dad," Matthew said, as he placed the steaks on the island next to his frantic wife.

"What's new buddy?" Robert responded.

"Boys, get in here and say goodnight to Pop."

"They not eating with us?" Robert questioned.

"They got a big day tomorrow and we could all use a meal without interruption for once," Sasha answered, now rushing from sink to island in final preparation for the meal.

"Where's old Sparky?" Robert questioned, quickly reflecting on his experience with the other pooch earlier.

"At the Vet, got a tract infection," Sasha replied.

"Poor buddy," Robert said. Thankful Sparky would not be attacking him this evening.

Sasha's erratic behavior began throwing off violent vibes and the sight of Matthew caused Robert concern. He usually came by at least twice a month for dinner but was summoned last week at some sense of urgency. Matty and Marco came bounding into the kitchen and strode up to their grandfather. Both giving him a small hug and then slowly shuffled off to their rooms with demonstrative bathroom instructions from Sasha. She finished her prep and set the table in a whirl while Matthew took up his seat across from his father.

"Did you fall into the shoe polish pop?" Matthew asked.

"Haahhhahahaha, nah, just started feeling like an old man. Trying to change things up a little bit," Robert responded.

"You look great dad; I mean you look ten years younger," Matthew said.

Robert nearly spit out some of the bland foreign ale, wanting to respond, actually twenty years younger but o.k.

"I told you the move to The Shores would be great for him," Sasha exclaimed, as she finally took her seat.

As they dug into the salad Robert's new eyes examined his host. Sasha was thinner than he had ever seen her. A proper beauty yes, but he never understood how his son could be satisfied with someone that looked like a walking coat hanger. She got her nails in him quick, causing Matthew to fall for her right after medical school. Mary nailed it from the jump. Sasha had a nice business degree of her own, but also had zero intentions of working a day of her life. Sasha hung at all the bars near Hopkins, she lassoed a promising cardiologist, affording her the lifestyle of gym workouts, home renovations, and high society functions. Robert and Mary tried to get Matthew to fish in the ocean before he settled, but a brunette betta beauty caught his lore and never let go. Glancing over at Matthew, Robert noticed he had put on at least twenty pounds, the swollen skin under his eyes signaled a stressed-out soul.

"Keeping busy boy?" Robert questioned, trying to break up the chewing silence that started the meal.

"Christ yeah, got to give it to you pops. Americans will always have heart disease. To think I wanted to be a primary physician. It is. Well, it's been a nonstop shit show the last few months," Matthew replied.

"You need to slow down boy. You can always switch fields. Make time for yourself and your family. Mom's passing should have been a trigger for you to realize that," Robert stated.

"It's not a good time for that now Robert," Sasha interrupted.

Robert cut into his steak, eyes glancing towards his son.

"Yeah pop, I have favor to ask you," Matthew said, nervously.

"What's that son?" Robert questioned. Taking a bite of his rare steak, surprised to actually get a bit of taste out of it, must be some remnants of blood from the cattle, Robert thought to himself.

"We need a loan. About fifty thousand," Matthew asked. His eyes concentrating on his food in attempt to not meet his fathers.

Robert chocked a bit on his meat and sat his fork down with authority. Then began.

"With the salary you make, how in the hell can you need money boy?"

"Robert, we have never come to you for anything. We just got a little behind and need a bridge loan to get us even for a while," Sasha interrupted again.

"You could go to work you know," Robert said, looking at Sasha.

"Really Robert," Do you know how much an Au Pair costs now? Running the boys to school, sports, not to mention proper tutors. Don't sit there and judge. Your grandchildren are top of their classes because I work with them. I put this house together, keep it spotless, I have your son's clothes prepared and meals cooked," Sasha replied, a sinical tone in her response.

"Well, there ya have it. I told you both not to buy this damn place. With interest what will you spend in the end. Four million on it? For what? Several rooms you never even use. Top of their classes? They are in elementary and middle school for Christ's sake," Robert shot back.

His host sat back in shock from Robert's aggressive response. He and Mary had advised but never got into his son's affairs. Robert knew they were living well above their means but figured Matthew had some sort of economic leash on his over exuberant wife.

"It's a different time Robert. Kids need constant supervision or do you not look at the world around you anymore. The dangers of it. Lecture me? Please. You saved your entire life for a rainy day that never came. You can't take it with you," Sasha replied. Taking a hateful long drink of her expensive chardonnay.

"Easy everyone. Dad look, it's just a loan. I am going to be on the board soon. With that comes more consultant money. We just got behind with the tuition and renovations to the house. That is all. To be fair, we did not ask for anything from the house," Matthew said, try to deescalate the situation.

"You mean your mother's and my house? That we paid off in ten years after purchase, same economic system I tried to explain to both of you. And did you not both go to Greece for three weeks this summer? I mean where does it end?" Robert exclaimed.

"Never mind, you know what Robert. Just keep it all and when you need to be moved again or need medical help to exist don't turn to us," Sasha said, as she got up grasping her empty plate with a clawed fist.

"When the fuck did I ask anyone to move? Short term memory loss must accompany laziness," Robert replied.

"Alright, Alright, everyone take a moment," Matthew demanded.

"I need to piss," Robert declared. He got up and headed to the upstairs bathroom to exit the escalating tense environment.

On his way up the stairs, a smile broke over the vampire's confident face. He always held back. At work when a director would needlessly push silly policies. On the ball field when a teammate would lecture on playing style. When it came to Sasha, he always just caved. It felt good, it felt damn good. A self-assured middle-aged man looked back at him in the bathroom mirror. A quick shock stole over him as he glanced down to see his fingernails an inch longer than they should be. Katie warned him to control his emotions. Quickly, Robert grinned in the mirror hoping not to see two protracted fangs, relieved he did not. Lifting the toilet seat, he started a gleeful piss. The clear liquid had a tint of red to it. Well fuck the fifty thousand they are going to get all of it Robert thought, believing this was the first sign of prostate cancer. He started to chuckle. It was just his new born body beginning to squirt out regenerated blood in a steady stream. He strode over to the sink to wash his hands out of habit and flicked the brass handle to the left. Warm water flowed loudly into the designer basin. Another sound interrupted the small waterfall. Robert shut off the water and held his head upward trying to detect the sound, the sound of a woman thrown in the heat of passion. With Matthew and Sasha downstairs who the hell was fucking their brains out? He exited the bathroom, tracking the sound next door to his oldest grandson's room. Placing his ear to the door, Robert could hear two distinct sounds. Some woman getting rode like a spirited race horse and a young man enjoying his new favorite toy. Robert backed away from the door quickly not wanting to interrupt his grandson's erotic evening.

Walking back downstairs he prayed the kid would keep his device lowered so his mother would not storm in on him, then thought of how the hell could he hear that over the pouring water. Once again remembering Katie's lecture on sense acceleration. Wishing his new found gift was discovered at a more appropriate time, he still stole a laugh before greeting his son back in the lobby.

"Come have a bourbon dad," Matthew kindly requested.

"Nah, I can't. Couple drinks these days knocks me off my ass. Look I'm sorry I came at you both so hard. It's been a rough adjustment. I'm just starting to feel like my old self. Are you In financial trouble son? I mean real financial trouble," Robert said.

"Not really. We might just downgrade the cars and cut back for a while. I know how you feel about the fancy stuff pop, but like Sasha said, it's a different world. You have to look the part," Matthew explained.

Robert put his hand on his son's shoulder and responded.

"No. No you don't son."

The two hugged and Robert made his way home. He weaved through the cul de sac, turned onto the main road, happy to leave the land of excess and pedicured lawns behind. Feeling great, he stopped at the liquor store before getting on the highway. Beer no longer had flavor, but he enjoyed the serenity of sipping on them anyway. A middle eastern man rung up the domestic sixer. Robert decide to purchase a small paper box of cigars as well. No cancer to worry about now. He thought a few beers along with a smoke would be a nice way to cap off the night. As the tanned man turned and crouched to the lower shelf, the new vampire picked up a scent. The man was afraid. Robert did not know of what or of whom, but this man was living in a constant state of fear. Katie's image bubbled up again, as her sweet voice explained that another gift would be that of scent emotion. Vamps can sniff out a mortal's sentimental spirit she had explained. Robert thanked the man, offering him a large kind smile, hoping it helped just a bit. That fucking bitch, he thought to himself as he reached his car. Placing the six pack and box of stogies on the roof, he then put both hands flat against the side of the car to steady himself from the horrid thought. Sasha had given off a strong scent. It was not that of embarrassment for asking for money. It was not that of rising anger of being put in her place. It was the stench of deceit. Mary was right all along, as usual. Sasha was betraying her family.

Chapter Six
October 6th

Unpacking the picture frames was always a tedious and frustrating task. Today, Robert was even more annoyed as he shredded through the styrofoam and brown paper that kept the glass safe. Rage pulsed through his undead body. Sasha. Sasha. Dammit he always knew it from the jump, so did Mary. That bitch was no good. Sasha's scent of betrayal seemingly clung in his nostrils, the odor seeping into his brain.

"Hey bud," Bruce whispered, making his way past Robert on his way to the bathroom. A full hour late today, but not under duress as Dawn had the day off.

Robert just shook his head hello, the thoughts of his son's cheating wife and the task at hand causing him too much coercion to speak. With anger clouding his performance, Robert clumsily took the fragile frames and tossed them without care onto the metal shelves. His focus shifted to Bruce returning to see what chore was next. The young man kept his windbreaker on though the temperature in the store hoovered around seventy.

"You o.k. bud?" Bruce questioned.

"Yeah, long night and they pack these cheap ass frames like they are a fucking Tiffany brand," Robert responded.

"Damn Yo, I never thought I'd hear you cuss," Bruce said. Nearly bursting with laughter.

"Yeah well, comes a time enough is enough."

"About time big Bob."

Robert agreed and started breaking down the pile of cardboard boxes, placing them in the cart to be carried off to the trash compactor. Bruce lazily helped by scoping up the foam intermittently between glancing at his phone, searching for a message that was not coming. The two made their way to the stockroom once the cart was filled with trash and the floor was cleared of all the debris.

"Damn boy, you coming down with a cold. Why are you still wearing your jacket?" Robert asked.

"This damn store is always chilly. Cheap ass owners control the thermostat," Bruce replied.

Robert did not need his new super senses to realize the kid was lying. The way Bruce grimaced as he tossed the soft cardboard into the green compactor caused Robert concern.

"Bullshit. Bullshit. Bullshit. Take it off," Robert gently demanded.

"It's all good dude, I'm fine," Bruce replied. Trying to mask his physical and emotional pain.

"Bruce, I'm not here to play your dad or judge, but let me have a look at whatever it is. I spent a lifetime in medicine. I just want to make sure you are alright. O.K. tough guy?" Robert pleaded.

Bruce nodded as he gingerly removed his windbreaker, squirming under pain when he removed the left side of the jacket as he lifted it over his head. Holding out his left arm, Bruce rolled up his tight undershirt, revealing his wound. A six-inch-deep purple bruise ran from Bruce's wrist down his forearm. The former nurse caressed the arm in both hands, slightly tilted it right to left. Bruce let out a grunt.

Robert took the kid's hand and closely examined the tops and bottoms of each finger. Using his own non protracted fingernail, he tapped each of the young man's nails with a strong flick.

"Welp, it's not broken, or you would be screaming right now. Looks like a bad sprain though. Gotta get it wrapped tight is all," Robert explained.

They walked to the employee bathroom which housed a basic first aid kit. Robert took out the brown wrapping and applied it to the injury while Bruce sat embarrassed on the toilet.

"How did this happen? And don't give me some I fell off my skateboard shit," Robert said.

With a small quiver bouncing from his lips, Bruce explained. "Kyle and I got into it last night. Just a little scuffle over money as usual."

"How bad is Kyle hurt?" Robert questioned. As he tightened the wrap to a seal around the thick part of the wrist. Just in time as well, the pulsing veins from the wound started to call out for him to nibble on.

After a moment of no response, Robert stood and leaned back against the sink, arms folded.

"I've seen some other marks on you kid. How long has this been going on?"

Bruce closed his eyes and small drops of water crept onto his cheeks.

Robert continued, "You got to leave him like today. I've seen this at the hospital a million times son. Does your family know?"

Eyes still closed, fighting back an eruption of tears, Bruce shook his head side to side signaling no.

"Do you want me to go with you to talk to them?" Robert asked.

"What family? My parents haven't spoken to me in two years until I get help for my "affliction" and my sister's husband won't let me around their house or their kids."

"Any close friends?" Robert asked. Careful to lower his voice to ease the tension.

"HAHHAHAHAA, all my friends are so doped up they don't know what day of the week it is."

Robert was a bit stunned. With the rainbow colored flags he saw at the ball games and the social justice warriors on full blast almost nightly on the news, he was blind to the fact that this kind of behavior still existed.

"There is always a solution. It starts by you leaving the situation asap," Robert said.

"And go where dude? I have no money. We live hand to mouth, and he barely works three days a week at the grocery store. I know, I know what you are going to say, but it's not that bad. Just. He drinks that fucking wine and goes ape shit time and again. I promise you most of our time together is great. He really looks out for me," Bruce explained.

Robert reflected on his training. Decades of dealing with abuse victims kicked in. He knew two things. One, nothing was going to be resolved right now. Two, this was going to continue until Bruce was either in the ER or dead. Robert put his hands on the young man's shoulders, he gave his friend a comforting smile.

"We will get through today and talk later. If you say you can handle it, fine. But I am always here to help and not just help by loading the heavy freight when your lazy ass doesn't want to," Robert said.

They shared a giggle. Bruce stood and gave his older buddy a hug.

The overhead speaker erupted and Debbie, between munching on some crunchy snack, called for one of the guys to check in a truck at the loading room. Robert told the kid to wash up and collect himself and went to the back to receive the shipment.

"Hey Pops, got six cases, count'em up would ya." A lanky delivery guy sprouted with too much pride for his slim frame. Robert just stared at him for a few seconds, then ignored the ignorance and eyed the count.

"Looks good slim, I'll take it from here," Robert said.

The delivery guy's eyes left his phone and swung towards Robert, gearing for a verbal assault.

"Ok, cool," The delivery guy responded.

When his eyes meet Robert's, confidence appeared to flood from his entire being. A frightened figure replaced an arrogant ass, quickly leaving sneaker skids as he walked with vigor back to his truck. A slight tremor rushed through Robert's hands. Bruce's abuse, delivery dick boy, the scent of Sasha's deceit still stagnant, all caused the violent transformation. Ten fingernails slightly elongated, quickly shooting two inches forward. Robert smacked the side of an empty shop cart, sending it flying to the far side of the stock room. After the cart spun to a halt, he closed his eyes in attempt to calm down. New images flashed past his closed lids. The fear filled look of the delivery guy and the cart rocketing against the wall with the slightest of touch. A slight smile replaced his angry mug as his new talons retracted. Robert strode from the backroom and back onto the sales floor with eerie confidence.

Two trucks loaded with furniture blocked the parking entrance to The Shores. All Robert wanted to do was warm up with a scolding shower before finding a game on the tube. With nothing on his plate, literally, for the next two days, some mind-numbing shows and sports seemed the perfect remedy for the frighting flu that was rampaging through his life. Putting the car in reverse, he three quartered turned and made way to the other side of the lot to park. Expecting the drain from the sun, there was welcomed relief as dusk had started to come early to announce the official arrival of autumn.

"BABA BOOEY!" a voice rang out, welcoming Robert to the lobby.

Instantly he knew who it was. Not only the vulgarity of the tone that echoed around the room but that fucking nickname. Bob.

Bobaroo. Bobby boy. All were welcomed variants of his name through the years. But only one man had called him, BABA BOOEY. Vito Vitalli. It could not be, but it was. Until Mary fell, Robert enjoyed his mortal existence in a garden of roses. Vito was the ugly thorn he could never pry out of his life. Early years were spent a few miles up the road in North Point. A blue-collar section of Southeast Baltimore county. A tight knit working-class community of perfect brick row homes that housed the hopes and dreams of the everyday American. Like so many small towns in the country, North Point had a few bad apples that spoiled the bunch. Vito came from one of those households. Vito was brought up as the kind of kid that cried favorites when not selected to the best sports teams. Blamed teachers when he failed courses and, in the end, bemoaned about the man shutting him down when fired from job after job. Vito spent most of his life hustling the bars, gambling, stealing, selling anything to anyone. Six kids and three wives later, it appeared that Vito was moving into his final home. Later, this brought on more rage from Robert. How can a man that lived such a life of debauchery end up in the same place as him? Another cruel hand delt from the stars.

"Hey Vito, good to see ya," Robert said. Walking slowly over to his old acquaintance with outstretched hand.

The two shook and Vito went in on a small man hug. Cheap aftershave filled Robert's oversensitive nostrils.

"Man, you live here now. Dis place is something ain't it?" Vito started.

"Yeah, been here a few months. Nice and quiet," Robert responded.

"My kid's wife been being a real bitch, so I had to get out of there. Department of aging got me a voucher. Only have to pay two hundie a month. Can you believe it, fucking government finally doing something for us working folks," Vito explained.

Angst and anger tumbled in Robert's belly, mixed parts Vito getting another handout and the stubby little man comparing himself to anything that resembles a working man.

Vito yelled another profanity at what looked like one of his grandkids about being careful with a piece of furniture, then started again.

"Did you know Tommy G and big Sal live here to?"

Robert did know that but responded, "Nah, I've been laying low since I moved in."

"I heard about your girl. Fuck, when your times up its up. Look I gotta make sure these assholes don't break my shit. Drinks tomorrow, we can catch up. Shit, it's gonna be like old times. Get with ya soon," Vito said. His curly white hair bounced off his fat neck as he went waddling after his help. And fuck, he was headed down the same hallway where Robert's unit was.

Rage once again slowly built at Robert's feet and coursed its way toward his head. Not wanting to walk behind Vito, he went into the mail room to check his box. Matthew had set his few bills to be automatically withdrawn so only coupons and religious pamphlets littered the small grey letter container. Sitting on the cushioned bench with an automobile coupon offering free tire rotations, Robert tried to center himself. The arrival of Vito stirred his old anxieties. Was he going to have to see this man every day? Was he going to have to loan him money? Was he going to have to share the comfort of his solidarity with the loud obnoxious degenerate? Shit, was he going to have to move again? Then comfort came over him like a soft cloud falling over a somber moon. He was immortal. Not sure how, when, or where, but he was going to be living somewhere forever. He was going to be spending time with a vampiric angel who just happened to be drop dead gorgeous. No need to fret, no need to get angry at the consistent flickering of misery cards that kept tumbling at him. Robert finally started to embrace his new gift and all the possibilities that came with it. A scent caught his attention, disrupting the joyful reflection. Something sweet, something delicious floated through the air of the mail room. Quickly getting up and rounding the corner, the sight before him was arousing, intoxicating, and horrific. One of Vito's crew had gashed their leg from broken shards of a mirror they were carrying. Thick blood poured down their calf, puddling into their socks. The blood called to him, the blood beckoned him, the blood yearned to him like a mother's breast to an infant. Heat broke out over his chilly skin, another rise begun in his work khakis, his gums went numb preparing for the arrival of newly formed fangs. Ignoring the quickly gathering crowd and loud profanities of the victim, Robert slowly jogged around the scene as he made haste to his home.

Chapter Seven
October 7th

Her blonde ponytail waived seductively behind her as Mary bounded toward him from the kitchen. Hands covered in cooking mittens, which held a perfectly baked warm cherry pie. Leaning over, she placed the desert on the T.V. tray in front of Robert and leaned in to kiss his forehead. Her firm breast playing peek-a- boo with his eyes as she worked her mouth to his ear and teasingly whispered her intentions. Mary headed back to the kitchen to clean up. Robert let the steaming pie cool as he watched the last few seconds of The Gong Show. His love had been radiating joy since her pregnancy was confirmed. Like most couples expecting their first, they were ecstatic, nervous, fearful, and ready to mask all of those emotions with nonstop sex. Ready to dig in, Robert picked up his utensils and slowly carved into the pie. Sweet cherry juice began to pour from the openings. Darker than usual, thicker than usual. A slow spread started to cover the entire top of the pie. More red juice, more thick crimson liquid started erupting from the small cut in the center. Robert dropped his utensils as the horrific vision caused him to panic. His eyes fixated on the odd occurrence. With no idea where all the juice was coming from, he turned his head to call for his wife. Mary stood in the hallway mouth open. A red fountain now cascading out of her open mouth onto the shag carpeting. BANG. BANG. BANG.

Catapulting from his laying position, Robert sat frozen for a moment. Frozen by the fear induced nightmare. Frozen by the incessant banging on his front door. Frozen by the slithering snake whipping its tail against hard glass.

"BaBa Booey, you home?" A familiar voice questioned from his closed entrance.

"Yeah! Just a sec," Robert responded. Trying to regain focus and reenter the real world from his horrific vision.

42

Sure as shit, not twenty-four hours after his arrival, Vito was at the front door. About to ask for a favor no doubt. Robert invited him in and headed to the kitchen to offer his unwanted guest a drink. Vito only came in a few feet before he began.

"Me and the boys are headed to the Lodge, I was seeing if you wanted to grab a few cold ones and catch up?"

A quick internal debate ensued. Head out with this crew for a bit or stay in and repeatedly go over Sasha's deceit, Bruce's domestic dilemma, his own transformation, and most likely have replaying visions of his dead wife vomiting blood. He told Vito he needed to wash up, but he would catch up with them at the bar.

"Cool brother, take care of that eye old man, looks like you got a bad scratch there," Vito said, before he headed out, slamming the door behind him like the disrespectful degenerate that he was.

Once in the bathroom, he saw what Vito meant. A quickly drying red stain sat just outside his left eye. A blood shed tear brought on by the horrific vision earlier no doubt. Robert centered himself in the steaming shower and made a mental note to try and enjoy a day out. Try not to focus on Vito's expected antics, try not to dwell on what he can no longer change. It would all work out once Katie returned. The three days since she left seemed like three months. A week and a half until her expected return, he had to just sit tight and try to embrace the last few days of some semblance of mortal existence.

Breathing corpses sat hunched at the bar at the Lodge. A stucco walled roadside tavern that was a fixture in the community since the 1950's. By the looks of the interior not much renovation had gone on since then as well. Wood paneled walls held posters of local sports teams as well as pictures of patrons passed. They did have flatscreens stapled in a row over the long bar, but no regular food on the menu. Domestic drafts, cheap liquor, and chips were how this old watering hole made its money. Of course, the machines that stood at attention along the back wall probably produced a steady source of income. That was where Vito was parked, his big ass hanging over the poor cushioned stool as he tried to outsmart the digital poker game. Robert, Tommy, and Sal sat at one of the tables going over the years as several frail gentlemen sipped gin and hacked phlegm at the bar. Tommy and Sal lived a little cleaner life than Vito, just a tad. Both worked and had families, both were divorced and remarried and had more family, then divorced again. A steady cycle of love, fuck, hate, repeat. Tommy looked closer to ninety than seventy, two bouts of cancer does that to a man. His thin frame looked barely strong enough to hold himself upright in his seat. Whatever weight Tommy did not have, Sal made up for. Robert estimated Sal close to three hundred pounds on his five-foot nine figure. Sal wore it well though, however his consistent removal and fumbling with his dentures was enough to nearly make anyone puke. Silently happy, Vito was fixated on the machine while Robert enjoyed the company of the other two. Tommy spent most of his time back and forth with checkups at the hospital. Sal watched his grandkids nearly every day, both seemed in good spirits. Only Sal had noticed Robert's physical state. Mentioning that he should just let his hair go natural, that all the ladies liked a snow-capped man these days. Robert laughed it off and made a gesturing remark about skin treatment he learned about during his years in the medical field that kept his face and skin looking decades clearer and tighter than it should. The conversation quickly moved to sports and why the hell the cheap ass owners will not buy any real talent when Vito went nuts.

"YEAH MOTHER FUCKER!" Vito hollered.

He hit, and from the sound of it, he hit big. Chubby hands pumping and his fat mouth yelping more cursed celebrations, one would have thought the man just hit the mega millions. As it was, twelve hundred was just about the same to Vito. After cashing in, and buying a round for the bar, the big man trolled over to his buddies.

"Alright boys, two words. Titty bar!" Vito exclaimed. Big smiles broke out over Sal's and Tommy's faces.

Robert forced a grin and tried to decline, stating he had to see his son in the morning.

"Fuck that noise, you're coming. We ain't no spring chickens BaBa Booey and we ain't gonna be round forever," Vito sprouted. Robert nearly replied, "Actually...," but refrained and agreed to come along to check out the show.

The boulevard of broken dreams consisted of two used car dealerships, one convenience store, two fast food joints, and three bikini bars. County ordinance prohibited full nudity and required pasties over the performer's nipples. Seductive underwear always stayed fastened to the dancer's bottoms, but bare breast jiggled on the stages of the clubs for four decades without a single complaint filed. Robert turned off the main road onto the gravel laced boulevard. Crunching rocks replaced smooth pavement as his car crept past the shops and clubs until Vito's truck flashed its right blinker, signaling right, and into the parking lot of Beavers. It had been an age since Robert had been to any of the clubs, usually a treat for when one of his teams took a championship or it was a teammate's birthday. Many a great time was had at the clubs, but Robert was never much into the entire strip club culture. Why eat a cheeseburger when he had prime rib at home. Not much had changed inside the club since his last visit. Red strobe lights surrounded an open cut bar with a ten-foot wooden stage placed in the center and a silver pole right in the middle going up to the ceiling. A middle-aged woman, that had seen better days, scurried from the register to the few patrons that were here before the night shift started. Night shift usually meant higher prices and better viewing options. The four gawking men that sipped their beers all looked older than Robert's group and were probably there to beat the expensive menu while hoping to glimpse a peek or two to relive old passions. Vito headed to the register to change his big bills into singles while Robert followed Sal and Tommy to the end of the long-circled bar. Never one to judge and always in admiration of anyone willing to part with their clothes for entertainment, Robert wore a grimace as he saw the dancer leave the jukebox and head to the stage. Blaring hip hop music with inaudible words blasted out as the young lady started a slow twirl around the pole. Tommy said something about the clubs not pulling chicks like they use to due to all the free internet porn and sites that let you have face to face dances online. Tommy kept ranting but Robert could barely make out anything he was saying over the music. Vito chatted up the bartender while Robert noticed he could count both the dancer's ribs and track marks. Diane, the bartender, made her way to the trio while Vito headed to another machine. Typical degenerate gambler that he was, a big score was not enough, he just had to keep playing. Diane poured the contents of a long bottle into three small muggy shot glasses, gingerly placing them in front of the guys. Robert was about to decline, then realized that he had finished a pitcher at the Lodge, yet he did not even have a slight buzz. No more watching how much he could drink and best of all, no more hangovers he supposed. The three toasted towards Vito, then downed the cloudy dark brown liquid. Robert made an educated guess that the shot was whiskey, but it tasted like tap water to him. Diane brought them three tall drafts as the dancer wrapped up her performance to a mild applause from the elderly crowd. She then started her sales pitch around the bar. The performer labored to get a twig sized leg up on the bar countertop where she would then open a flappy garter belt that invited crumpled bills. Sal struggled to tip the performer as his belly did not allow him to reach to the end of the bar to slide the single into her belt. Laughing, he stood up and slid his chubby hand down her leg to place his economic appreciation. Last time Robert was here, that would have got a customer booted or perhaps a crack to the jaw. Her dilated eyes barely flinched as she slid her leg toward Tommy. He and Robert tipped the emaciated performer as she made way back toward the restroom. Only the sounds of clinking glasses from Diane and the wheezing breathing of the older crowd filled the room. A shout followed by a couple pings came from Vito's way, signaling another hit. The next rail thin dancer came from behind them. She stumbled toward the jukebox to select her song. It did not take many years of treating O.D.S. for Robert to notice a reoccurring trend. These girls were all dancing to fix up and fixing up to be brave enough to dance. He had seen the cycle before, yet still empathized with their plight. Sal said something along the lines that he had bigger tits than these girls when a warm hand fell upon Robert's cool shoulder.

"Hey stud, your friend bought you dance. Come with me," The girl said.

Robert snapped his head to the left, getting an undead eyeful of the woman that stood beside him. Moon tattoos ran up and down her arms, around her thick thighs, and in between her two big breasts.

"BABA BOOEYYYY!" Yelled Vito, from his machine.

Tommy, Sal, and the few other patrons joined in with a hoot and holler.

She took Robert's hand, leading him back towards the back of the building. They passed the restrooms and went through a wooden sliding door that held an Employees Only sign in the center. Dancer one and some other girls glared at the couple as they walked past their dressing area and through another door. The small space beyond the door had a green loveseat, glass table, and wall length mirrors on three sides of the wood paneled room. Lap dancing was also against the law in this part of town, but Robert was sure no one complained about that either. From what he smelled from the sofa, more than bump and grind went on back here.

"I'm Luna. Take a seat, get comfy, we can go when the next song plays," Luna explained.

With no idea what was coming next, Robert quietly just sat in the middle of the loveseat and tried hard to think of something to say. Before he could utter a word, hard rock blasted through the building as the next dancer probably took her cue. In response Luna tore off her top. She twirled several times in front of him, each circle giving a nice snapshot of her two perfect tits rising above and below her painted moon. With her back to him, Luna pulled her hair up, revealing another moon on the back of her neck, she let her pitch-black hair fall past her shoulders. Luna then bent forward putting her plump ass right onto Robert's knees. He got his first heat surge looking at her milky white cheeks. Spreading her legs, she mounted him backwards and started to grind. Moments later she stood again, mounting him from the front, putting her hands around his head and shoving his face right in between her large white breast. The heat started to burst inside him. His hands lay flat on both sides of him, they both started to twitch. His gums went numb again. As Luna bounced each tit on the side of his cheeks, Robert puckered his lips inward, trying to fight off the incoming fangs. He had a few lap dances in his time, but this session was getting heated quick. Luna was not just putting in a shift, she started full on riding him like a wild cowgirl on top of a bull at a rodeo. About to full on turn, the music stopped. Luna placed her hands on his shoulders, leaned back and attempted to catch her breath.

"Damn. Shit. Sorry. I don't know what got into me," Luna apologized.

"No problem, that was great. Thank you," Robert replied, wanting her off him before he lost control and bite deep into her heavy chest, which was all he could think about doing at the moment. Luna dismounted her stallion.

"It's thirty a dance, sixty for three, and for a hundred we can have some real fun."

"Next time for sure, I'm a little strapped this week."

"No sweat, I work days Tuesdays and Thursdays. That's best, night shift is always too busy to have real fun. Bring a hundie next time stud."

She put her top on, opened the narrow door, and headed back to the bar, not before giving Robert one last longing look. That was no look of thanks, it was the look of lust. Rule of five Robert remembered briefly; the sexual allure was part of it. He made a motor boat sound with his lips and started to get up when he noticed a wet red spot on his zipper. Old Robert would have regurgitated at Luna's leak. New Robert stared at the rose-colored droplet with desire. Water formed at the corners of his mouth as he salivated. He wanted to bite those breast as they bounced in front of him, but he craved the taste of the red liquid that sat below him. No longer able to resist, the thirsty vampire swooped the droplet into his middle finger, jamming it into his eager mouth. He sucked on his finger like a starving lion would to a gazelle's neck. There was a twenty-dollar shot at one of the bars that ran across the beach in Sarasota, Robert had to try it. The bourbon exploded in his throat, shooting heated adrenaline through his body. Mary mimicked his face the rest of that vacation. The finger food he just inhaled gave triple that effect. His muscles tightened, his body pulsed, his chest filled with joy and strength. He used his tongue to rub the small remnants around the roof of his mouth. Pure ecstasy filled his jaws. The mouse tasted ok, Katie had said that she diluted the small sample she gave him from her shoulder to tide him over. Katie also said that human blood from different parts of the body gave different effect. It was obvious that a drip from a woman's best kept secret was as potent as crack was to an addict. Katie also said do not even think of even taking a taste until she could train him. He understood now.

"Hey, I need the room dude," Dancer one said. Tommy giggling behind her.

"Ugh, Yeah, Sure, Sorry," Robert replied. Shook out of his blood induced daze.

"Tore it up huh Bob?" Tommy said.

Robert winked at him, then hurried out of the small room, past the room of dancers, all of whom had their eyes dancing frantically into their cells, and out to the bar. Luna was bouncing her breast on both sides of the pole as the crowd cheered over the sound of some quick paced country song. She caught his eye for a second, instantly grinning nearly ear to ear. Sal was sitting with another dancer. Robert gave them a quick wave and headed over to Vito. The big man was riding a hot streak. Robert nearly had to shout over the music.

"Thanks for the dance man, I really got to get going."

"No problem buddy. Damn already, it's not even eight and the good chicks get here soon," Vito replied. Eyes following the bouncing cherries floating up and down on the machine monitor.

"Yeah, running to do tomorrow and going to see my boy. I had a great time," Robert shouted.

"First of many my friend, first of many," Vito explained.

Robert gave him a pat on the back and made his way past a group of young men that just came in. They were all wearing neon yellow vest, the universal uniform of all the dockworkers. Coming in to sneak in one cheap beer before the more expensive menu hit the tabs and more expensive women hit the stage. Robert turned at the door, he stole one last glance at Luna as she wrapped up her performance. His eyes lasered between her thighs, wanting, craving, salivating.

Chapter Eight
October 8th

Around four AM the blood high wore off. An over energetic man was shouting through the television, encouraging the Viewer to take hold of their physical fitness. That tiny little drop of blood had Robert wired all night. His muscles stayed tightened, his eyes would not shut, his tongue roamed the inside of his mouth for hours. Wanting to recapture that tantalizing taste. It was the taste of life itself. His body held a slight ecstasy quiver from the moment he left the bar until now. Slowly trembling minute by minute with only the thought of the drink on his mind, like a decade old alcoholic that just went their first day without a sip. The wired new vampire tried focusing on old sitcoms that played on the flatscreen and attempted to play a game on his phone that Bruce set up for him. Nothing could keep his attention longer than a few minutes before Robert would return to a trance like state. Sitting straight up on the sofa, just replaying the explosive joy of that finger licked lust. Making love to his perfect partner, striking down a batter to win a championship game, the rushes he got from resuscitating near dead patients made Robert no stranger to euphoric emotions. The taste of the woman's blood was something altogether from another realm. Derived from another dimension of physical and spiritual consciousness. Several times during his career, blood had splattered around his mouth, of course he had kissed a few splinters and small cut wounds from both his wife and son. On those occasions he, like most mortals, would get a sweet thick treat that was usually spat out instantaneously. This new nocturnal biological system seemed to not only need, but cherish, no crave, human's vital fluid. Reason swept over him as the blood buzz finally dissipated. He had an agenda today. The very human emotion of anger washed over his fleeting ecstatic state, returning him to the mortal world. Still five hours until the bank opened, Robert went over to his small two-seater dinette set and pulled out a notebook from under a two-day old newspaper. Removing the pen from the wired inseam, he popped open the lined padded book and wrote down his plan. This was another old habit that helped immensely for concentration and focus. Thirty minutes later he reviewed his strategy and starred at the last phrase written on the small pad. HELP MATTHEW ECONOMICALLY AND EMOTIONALLY AT ALL COST.

Too much had clouded his mind, of course he would have to meet with the branch manager for a withdraw of this magnitude. Only in a bank can one be made to feel guilty for taking their own money. Robert swore they made these thin cushioned seats uncomfortable on purpose. He stopped squirming as the plump woman entered her tight office with a security guard in tow. Shiny but cheap jewelry hung from her ears and around her neck. Grey in color, but Robert was thankful for lack of taste, obviously all of the pieces were not real silver. The tall guard stood proud as a peacock at the gap in the door, dressed impeccably but not with any weapons that those night eyes could see. Small local branch, no real criminal would take a pop at this place.

"Sorry for the delay Mr. Robinson, for a withdraw of this magnitude, we need to ask a few questions. To protect you of course," Barbara said. Never properly introducing herself but the large nameplate that sat on her desk did the deed.

"Not a problem at all. I appreciate the concern," Robert replied.

"Just a few questions," Barbara said again. Her eyes left Robert's and went to the guard. In response the guard turned and blocked the entire open entrance of the office with his large frame.

"Are you currently being harassed to make any form of payment to an individual or debt collector?" Barbara asked.

"Nope," Robert answered.

"Are you currently under any medically prescribed drugs that could alter your decision making?"

"Nope."

His brief answers causing her to break stride and shoot a glare at her customer. Her eyes, small beads that sunk beneath bad purple mascara. She took a deep breath and started again.

"Are you currently under the influence of any alcohol or narcotics."

"Nope," Robert answered. This time with a chuckle accompanying his response.

"Mr. Robinson, we take great responsibility in…" Barbara started, before Robert cut her off.

"Barbara. I get the questions. I feel good, no I feel great. I've been at this bank for over thirty years. Let me save you some breath. The money is for my son and his family. Now I have some appointments today. So please hand me my cashier's check and tell big boy to take a break."

Barbara reluctantly leaned forward with an envelope containing the check. She gave it a little clutch before he removed it from her pudgy grasp. Rising and making his way past the guard, Robert could hear the big man's heart start to race. Say something son the vampire mimed to himself. The guard started to mug Robert as he strolled past him. Robert shot a stare into the man's pupils causing him to take a clumsy step back and nearly stumble through the glass door. Smiling, the powerful undead man strutted with confidence out of the bank, he was starting to really embrace his new life.

Only Sasha's car sat parked in the long driveway, Robert was thankful for that. The boys would be at school, he assumed Matthew would be at the hospital. He needed to see her alone, he needed to be sure. With no idea how his new gifts worked, he slowly began to learn on the fly. The deceit that reeked from his last encounter with Sasha, the foul fear from the liquor store clerk, and Barbara. What was it? She gave off a nervous scent as she spat out her standard operating procedures. Bank must be in trouble if one large withdraw caused that paranoid perspiration from the boss lady. He could hear Sasha scattering around the living room, chatting loudly on the phone. Robert composed himself before ringing the fancy door bell. Moments later his daughter-in-law opened the door. A surprised expression plastered on her chiseled face. She waived him in and hit a button on the large phone.

"Hi Bob, shoot, can you take a seat in the living room? I'm just wrapping up a call."

"Sure, take your time, all I have is time," Robert said.

Sasha smiled and made haste through the oval greeting room toward the back of the house. Obviously wanting to be out of earshot. Robert shook his head as he strolled into the living room, grabbing the closest seat. The chair was white leather and probably cost more than his first car. A rapid small laugh exited his mouth. His entire plan had gone to shit. He knew everything he had to in ten seconds. Expecting her to be shocked by his unannounced arrival, she was more than that. She was embarrassed, she was a tad frightened, most of all she was caught. Perking up his head quickly, Robert knew something else. She was on the phone with him now. The rumbling of the dryer muffled her conversation, but the keen vampire concentrated and made out some of the conversation. Sasha was more than clever as she pitched her voice, making it to sound like she was talking to a girlfriend or fellow soccer mom.

"Yeah, Monday works great. Yup, after my work out. Sounds great, can't wait."

She hung up and was at a near sprint back to Robert, not before asking him if he wanted anything to drink on her way through the kitchen. He declined and a second later she bounded into the sitting room, her straight dark brown hair in disarray.

"Shoot you just missed Matthew. He has an early surgery today," She said. Leaning on the full chaise across from Robert.

"Actually, I was hoping to just speak with you and hand you this," Robert said. Taking the envelope from inside his coat pocket and reaching it out to her. Wanting her to come close, so he could get a whiff.

Sasha took the white envelope and slowly opened it as she made her way back to the chaise to sit. The lying bitch reeked of lies and betrayal, it smelled like sour lemons. Her eyes exploded at the sight of the check.

"Bob, we can't take this. This is twice what we asked for and really, we can make do right now. It was just. Well just. The house went for a lot more than all of us expected. A little boost would have helped around here. But seriously, we can't take this," She said.

Robert did not need any supernatural senses to know that she had no intention of giving it back, though her performance was admirable.

"Nah, you were right. Can't take it with me. With Mary gone, you four are all I got left. I've seen enough families torn apart in the E.R to know anything can happen. But I've got plenty and you both deserve the best. So, I insist you take it," Robert explained. Subtle rage started brewing in his belly again as he rose to make for a polite but quick exit. His daughter by marriage stunk of diabolical duplicity. Sasha stood and came in for a hug. The physical contact almost triggered a transformation. Making their way to the front door, Robert regained his purpose and asked.

"I couldn't help but overhear ya a bit on the phone. What gym do you go to? They got a program at the senior center, but I can't even break a sweat with what they do, besides the fact that it smells like piss and hard candy in there."

Sasha smiled, attempting to hide the surprised quiver that was rattling her bottom lip.

"Oh, Oh, it's in the mall. But it's a really intense place. Lots of meatheads and adrenaline junkies. There is a place down your way. Fit As A Fiddle. Nice little spot for a good work out. I think they have a program geared for seniors."

"I'll have to give it a look on my way home. Tell Matthew I will call him soon. Tell him not to make a big deal out of the money either," Robert said. They exchanged another small hug. Robert set off with all the information and evidence he needed.

The ride home was tough. A summer sun snuck into October, the glare radiated through the front windshield, draining the vampire of energy. Thinking fresh air would help a bit, Robert hit the button to his left, prompting the window to slowly scroll down. The air helped a bit when he hit the highway, but extreme weariness began to settle in. Off the exit, at the first light on the main road home, not just the sun but the day's events took its toll. Katie spoke of never needing to worry about money again, even if immortality was not gifted to him, there was plenty of reserve to last him another fifty years if need be. But the realization that he just withdrew one-hundred-thousand dollars and handed it over put a morose mask over his mortal rational. Then Sasha. Holy shit Sasha. Busted six ways to Sunday. Robert had hoped to get a little information from her before slowly bringing Matthew into the fold, but now he could call her full out. Not sure yet how to go about it, he knew that his son had to know. Life was short. Too damn short to work so damn hard only to get it ripped from you one penny and betrayal at a time. Too many of his friends hit their fifties penniless and heartbroken for him to see it happen to his boy. The entrance to the Shores came into sight just in time, just before the exhausted vampire nearly passed out behind the wheel. Robert slugged out of his car and limped toward the entrance of the community. Sliding glass doors parted as the dim lobby lighting brought slight relief to the vampire's weary undead soul.

Cackling from the old hens that nested in the media room exploded into his ears. Gossip of church, fellow residents, and economics rattled out of their mouths, catapulting into Robert's oversensitive mind. A strange desire coursed through the vampire, the desire to stroll into that room and drain each of those worthless women of every drop of their precious blood. Robert was grateful that the desire faded with each step he took away from their babbling. He needed to rest. He needed to think. And the dry sensation that ran through his throat meant he needed to drink.

Chapter Nine
October 9th

Saturdays were always a living nightmare at Dollar Land, but this Saturday was a shit storm from hell. The four-hour short shift felt longer than one of Robert's old twelve-hour nights at the hospital. Everything that could happen in the world of cheap retail, did. The entire fridge system had gone bad in the night. Dawn's fury rose above the stench of spoiled milk and cheap meats that were encased in the now warm glass covered walls. Hopeful for a leisurely morning of restocking the chariots of carts that sat idle behind the registers, Robert had to now empty the entire wall of frozen goods as well as documenting the inventory of the large loss. As if loading melted ice cream treats and reeking baloney packages was not enough, Dawn's eternal Saturday rampage routine rang through his skull. Each tirade a sharp stake to his temple.

"Can't they at least front face one fucking aisle? How hard is it put a cart or two of returns back? If one of these counts is short, it's coming out of their pay! I'm sick of this shit! Can't Bruce get his skinny ass here on time, one fucking day!" Dawn shouted.

Robert felt a tear in the cardboard. He glanced down to see a slit in the tough brown box. His nails had extended into tiny sharp knives causing him to pierce through two-dollar pizza boxes. Usually, he and Bruce would be having a giggle at Dawn's weekly wailing, but today it incited rage in the old new vampire. Robert wanted to bellow, "Bitch, it's every week with you. These kids barely make over minimum wage. Half of them are stoned at work. Do you actually think in over twenty years anything will change?"

Instead, he closed his eyes in desperate attempt to relax. A small hum buzzed through the freezer doors as all the lights inside flickered on one by one. He could hear Debbie give a shout of joy from the front of the store. Half an hour later the now cooling freezers were up and running but sat empty. After loading the last U boat of rotted goods in the back, Robert opened one of the frosty doors so he could pop his head in for a minute. The blast of frigid air felt fantastic against heated skin. Calmed down and cool, he heard the front door to the store ping as the Saturday crowd poured through the entrance like mad cows. This signaled an hour had past and still no Bruce. No time to worry as the questions flew at him.

"Where's all the milk? Is there any orange juice in the back? Do you expect a shipment today? How come there was nothing put on your website about the frozen foods being out?" they roared like roosters without heads. Robert took the bulk of the questions on the floor while Dawn faced the fury at the front of the store.

"The circular said 2 for 1 pizza! I spent gas money getting here! How are you going to compensate me! What is your corporate number! I want to speak to the higher higher ups! You won't get my money ever again!" They shouted with uneducated confident glee. Dawn spat back with fire. "How the hell could we know the system would go down until we got here! Do you want to eat spoiled meat! I am the higher higher up!"

Robert had no idea whether to laugh or cry. The sad state of moral decay was horrifyingly depressing. The comedic dialogue was fit for a sitcom special. Like most of America, there was another Dollar Land not five minutes away. Corporate? In the few months he had been here, not a single call or visit from anything resembling a corporate office had taken place. He assumed they just sat back and collected. As long as no one died in the store, who the hell would argue or get emotional over cheap goods that had to be purchased in bulk by pennies on the dollar. After the initial battle subsided, Robert was instructed by a flustered boss to just stock seasonal today and tidy up as best as possible. Unlike the slower weekdays, Saturdays were tough to get product out. The aisles were cramped with customers and radiated with human heat. He stole a quick break in the restroom so he could run cool water over his heated hands, then wiped some on his face. Another glance in the mirror was a bit shocking. A younger stranger stared back at him. His newly formed face was something he was going to have to get used to, Robert could not believe that no one had taken a more dramatic look at this rapid youthful transformation. He chalked it up to perhaps everyone thinking he was finally over the long mourning first stage and ready to get back to living life. Another quick glance at his watch signaled just two hours left in this shitty shift. Still no Bruce. Stacking the seasonal freight into a cart, it was too crowded to haul the bulky U boat on the floor, Robert began to worry about his little buddy. Back on the floor he waltzed around customers who stared at products like they were artistic masterpieces hung in a museum. Robert methodically started to open and stock the seasonal goods. Halloween of course. Next to Christmas, Halloween was Mary and his favorite holiday. So many memories of little Matthew galloping through town as a cowboy, police officer, and various monsters. Memories of adult parties that got a little rowdy for the conservative couple but was all in fun. October nights cuddled with Mary under a warm blanket watching the best of Romero, Craven, Carpenter, enjoying all the masters of the macabre. With all that had happened in the last week he had not once taken notice of the holiday. As per the new retail wave, they had been stacking cheap pumpkin pales and plastic costume mask since August. Almost fatefully, the first product out of the box was a vampire snow globe. A small castle stood over the tiny smiling cartoon vampire figure. Robert gave it a little shake which sent red flakes dancing around the grinning creature. He removed a dozen more, then placed them with care under the ten-dollar sticker. Big ticket item in this store. Stepping away from the newly shelved bobbles, he thought about what kind of vampire he would be. Mary always loved the reluctant Louis from that film with Brad Pitt, or was her passion from the book by Rice? Robert's favorite portrayal of the famous monster was Christopher Lee as Dracula. The iconic actor perfectly personified the classy yet deadly count. Would he himself be classy? Would he be reluctant, or would he succumb to the calling of the blood? One tiny drop had nearly driven him mad. Katie would know. How much longer? Another week? Ten days? How could she leave him in this state of transformation? Was he going to make it until she got back? She instructed him to lay low, leave his job, fake the flu. Robert felt sitting on a sofa with only a corn snake for company would be ten times worse than just drifting around until she came back. He was wrong. Already nibbling the forbidden fruit, uncovering a dark family secret, as well as having several physical outbreaks brought on by strong emotion. THUMP!

A cry burst out to his left. While he was overthinking the current state of affairs, a small child had sprinted into his thigh while running laps around the store. The child had bounced off of his strong leg and hit the laminate floor hard.

"Hey there, you ok buddy?" Robert asked, offering comfort to the child.

"What the hell did you do mister?" An angry mother spat at him as she rounded the end of the aisle, marching with fury towards her hysterical son.

"Little guy just ran into me, that's all," Robert explained.

The mother grasped one of the child's arms and yanked him up like a dog owner pulling on the leash of a rabid pooch. "I told your ass stop running round this store!" she then proceeded to bend the child over and whack him several times.

"Whoa, whoa, he didn't do any harm. Kids run through the aisles all the time. You should see my grandkids at the mall," Robert said. Trying to calm the abusive mother.

"Mind ya damn business pops!" The mother shouted back.

"NO! MIND YOUR FUCKING CHILD LADY!" Robert replied. His usually soft voice replaced by that of a dark demon.

The child went dead silent, the woman staggered back with kid in tow. Her anger was quickly replaced with fear. Her forward march became a quick back pedal as she fled toward the back of the aisle, around the corner and out of the store quickly. Oldman from the Coppola adaption. Yup. That was who Robert would mimic. A sophisticated classy vampire who on a dime could stamp his undead foot, unleashing the fires of hell. It was settled, that was the vampire he would be.

Like all bad things, the shift finally came to an end. Four employees sat in the small lounge area gazing at their phones before their shift started. Robert made way to the small computer and logged in to punch out. A quick scattering ensued as Dawn stormed into the lounge. "Let's get at it!" she shouted. In response, the young kids scurried to their registrars and points of assignments.

"No word from Bruce?" Robert asked, as he punched out for the day, standing to face his flustered boss.

"None. I'm damned worried Bobby. He's always late, but not once has the boy never no called, no showed. Never. I'd head over to his house, but I'm here all day. We got an emergency truck coming to restock the fridge. If he doesn't post tomorrow, I will check in on him. Thanks for all your help today. If you ever want that keyholder position it's yours," Dawn said, then headed back to the floor, ready to tackle the next emergency.

Robert admired her. It takes a strong person to care about a place that no one else does. Quickly putting on his windbreaker over the cotton employee polo, the tired employee flew out of the store. A smile of gratitude sprung upon his pale face as a cloudy autumn afternoon covered the sun.

Tan leaves littered the long driveway that introduced Merritt Trailer Park. Large bare trees hovered over the twenty odd mobile homes like judging mothers. The humble tiny homes had seen better days. The mobile park reeked of pot, alcohol, and poverty. Very young and very old adults resided in the rental community. Still, the beauty of October surrounded the junk cars, broken toys, and cheap plastic furniture that were scattered through the small lawns. Robert had taken Bruce home several times after shifts when he had to stay late to stock bigger shipments. Bruce not calling or texting caused him concern. Even if he went on a full-on bender, the kid would have at least sent a text, for not wanting to hear the dressing down from Dawn. Bruce and Kyle's home sat last house on the left of the dead-end street. An older ford truck was up on the grass, parked too close to the wooden steps that led to the front door. Robert pulled up properly parallel to the ford and turned off the car. He took out his phone to check one more time to see if Bruce had replied to any of his text. Only Matthew's thank you emoji, which was sent late in the night, popped up under the phone's message icon. Robert exited the car, then slowly strolled up to the plastic front door screen. He wrapped strongly, hoping to wake Bruce in case he had simply just overslept. A few more wraps and minutes later, Robert walked to the far end of the front deck and tried to pear in through the windows. Cheap curtains blocked out any view inside, but one window was half open. A scent fluttered from the inside. Strong wine mixed with stale blood. The front door creaked open, a heavily tattooed young man staggered out, covering his eyes from a sun that was hiding behind autumn clouds.

"What's up yo?" the clearly inebriated man child questioned.

"Hi, is Bruce around? I work with him," Robert asked.

"Nah, he took off last night."

"Are you Kyle?"

Kyle started a smoker's cough and hocked up a tremendous spit before answering. "Yeah Yo. Hit him up on his cell, I don't know where he went." Kyle turned to head back in attempt to sleep off the obvious hangover. Before he could shut the screen door Robert was next to him in unnatural speed.

"Let's have a little chat son," Robert said, placing his strong hand on Kyle's shoulder.

"Da fuck man. I said I don't know where he is," Kyle pleaded, nearly shocked sober by the illusion of Robert moving five yards in a frightening flash.

With one hand upon Kyle's shoulder, Robert forcefully guided Kyle into the house, released him, then slammed the door shut behind them. The door creaked and split one hinge by the force. The stench of cheap wine was nauseating, but the odor of dried blood caused the vampire personal excitement as well as quick concern for his friend. Kyle, coughing again, parked himself on a beer-stained loveseat. Sizing up Bruce's lover, Robert really felt bad for his friend. Kyle had a protruding belly, unhealthy pale skin, and reeked of despair.

"Where's he at Kyle?" Robert asked boldly.

"Dude, we got into it last night and he bolted. I have no idea. Probably his parents," Kyle muttered back.

"Why is there blood on the carpet Kyle?" Robert questioned, anger building in his stomach.

"What da fuck yo, when were you in our bedroom?"

In a flash, Robert bolted towards Kyle. With immortal strength he pinned Kyle's shoulders to the top of the sofa with clawed hands. Kyle froze in fear, his blood shot eyes held by two black pupils seeing deep into his soul.

"WHAT THE FUCK HAPPENED HERE LAST NIGHT KYLE?" Robert bellowed, softly but with a voice that was unfamiliar to the frightened little boy that sat stapled to a now pissed stained cushions.

From a quivering lip, Kyle responded, "I quit my job yesterday. He got all pissy and we got into it. I popped him in his nose then he took off. I swear sir, that's it."

Robert, staring down at the frightened flesh puppet whispered, "You ever lay a hand on him again and …"

Shooting his head forward to meet Kyle's, Robert exposed his fangs and hissed. Accompanying the hiss was a hot phlegm filled spit that covered Kyle's forehead. Now crying, the young man closed his eyes. After feeling the death grip let loose on his shoulders, Kyle cautiously forced his lids open. The front door was wide open, the screen door swayed in the fall wind. After hearing the engine start just outside the trailer, Kyle sprinted to the open front door to watch his attacker flee the community.

Chapter Ten
October 10th

Six days, Seven days, how long was he supposed to go without feeding? Robert could not remember, nor could he think straight with the thirst pounding in his throat. During busy nights at the hospital, he had gone long shifts without eating and his stomach would rumble on the early morning ride home. The new vampire concluded it was the throat that bore hunger pains for vampires. An hour earlier his entire neck had swelled as the desire to feed clouded all of reality. Nothing else mattered. Robert reread his dark life template form, then headed to the pet store. Quickly peeking in on the snake who seemed at ease. A few tiny bird eggs every couple days kept the slimy bastard docile.

Wood shavings from the hamster cages and fish piss appeared to cascade over Robert, burning his nostrils with their heavy scents. He felt tired. He felt weak. His eyelids fluttered as the thirst began to dominate his physical life force.

"Hi, I need two white-footed mice please," Robert whispered to the young woman who stood at the service center twirling her purple hair.

"Alive or frozen?" she responded.

"Alive," Robert answered. He placed both of his hands on the counter to hold himself up.

"What kind of reptile do you have? Frozen is much better..." The associate tried to explain before being cut off.

"Just get the fucking mice please little girl," Robert demanded. The words came out soft but deep. Ms. purple streaks shot off a snare then scurried to retrieve the rodents. She quickly returned with a white feeder bag that had two tense mice frantically squeaking in duress. Robert inserted his debit card. The emaciated vampire nearly fell down as the payment processed.

"Sorry dude, I have a Boa. Was just trying to give some advice. I'd love to see your snake some time," She explained, with a gleam in her eyes.

Robert just removed the card once it said approved, then snatched the bag, exiting the store without a response but thinking, not even in my drunkest state sweetheart.

Sitting in his car, with the squealing puncturing his sensitive ears, Robert tried to remember Katie's instructions. He wanted to wait until he got home but the thumping in his throat vibrated his esophagus. Checking the mirrors and around the car first, he took a pen from the console and tried to pierce his palm. The intended result was not achieved. Instead, a blue scribble mark made its way from his pointer finger to his thumb. He tried again. This time the pen bent against his tough skin. Robert tilted his head back and let out a steady stream of vulgarities. Thoughts turned to Sasha. Katie had said he could bring on the change with imagery of lust, love, but pure hate worked the best. Sasha's sinister smile got him going, then Kyle. He pictured Kyle putting his hands on Bruce. The heat came quick. This time Robert let it take over. Opening his eyes, the image in the dashboard mirror reflected a monster. Brown pupils went full on black. He gave the mirror a smile revealing two small ivory knives that hung from his gums. Wanting to drink quickly to calm the quivering, clumsy clawed hands attempted to unfasten the plastic top to the bag. This proved a struggle with those long sharp nails protruding from the meaty tips of his fingers. Finally, he just cut a slit in the top of the bag and pulled out the frightened mouse. Another glance around the near empty parking lot announced that the coast was clear to have an early morning sip. Katie showed him how to gently slit the side of the furry neck to get the most out of the rodent. With all the grace and experience of a professional nurse, Robert took to the task at ease as his steady hands made a tiny incision. Sipping slowly on the wound, the vampire's strength and focus returned nearly immediately. Fuzzy white fur from his meal made him sneeze, in response, red droplets flew from his nose onto the steering wheel. Holding the drained rodent down to his right, he leaned back and started to laugh. Wow, he thought to himself. His eyes could see the tag numbers from other cars fifty yards away. His fit form returned at once replacing the tired man that had pulled into the lot a ten minutes ago. All of that from one little nibble from a mouse he thought, then remembering the tiny drop from Luna and the half shooter Katie had given him from her body. It was a thousand times more potent than the adrenaline shots he had administered to next to death patients. The engine kicked over, and Robert placed the deceased mouse back in the bag with his soon to follow companion. The blood call was still there. Should he just go ahead and take another nibble? What would be the harm of that? Would he vamp out and go rampaging through the parking lot? Would he return to the store and get a slice of purple pie? Heat. The sun broke through the early morning clouds, seeped through the windshield, and started to slightly burn his neck. He stole another look in the mirror, a handsome middle-aged man smiled back. Pulling around the back of the parking lot more answers started to replace questions. He showed resounding restraint in not ripping Kyle to pieces yesterday. Today he was at near starvation. He just filled himself up and desired more instantly. One drop from Luna sent him into a blood drunk daze. It was coming together, but he still yearned for Katie's return. So many mortal questions still to answer. How was he going to fake his death? How long could he keep in touch with his son and grandkids? Where were they going to live? HOOOOONNNKKKK.

An angry driver behind him laid on their horn as Robert noticed that his question-and-answer session ran through an entire light that returned to his new favorite color. Red. The angry driver was spitting fire in his reflection mirror. Do not make me get out of this car little man, he mumbled to himself with a grin.

Three of spades was the card. Four of a kind and a sure winner. For the first time in hours a sly grin broke over the worried vampire's fresh face. Over a couple beers, he had returned to his apartment and plotted his Sasha stalking session for tomorrow night with renewed focus. The drum beating on the door signaled Vito's return. The fix was in. Robert had to know it would only be a matter of time. The fat man had already set up a steady Sunday night game in the media room area. BABA BOOEY would sit with Tommy, Sal, alongside another insider while Vito would oversee four other tables of saps. It was useless to resist him and how much longer would Robert really have to be here anyway. Strawberry cough drops and cheap gin filled the air of the room where eager retirees looked to double their monthly checks. Sure enough, Vito had five tables in all, filled with slightly buzzed seniors ready to hit it big on Vito's Vegas night at the Shores. Robert had to give it to him. There were fake money bills ready for exchange, beer and liquor lined up on the plastic side tables that sat with bowls filled with soft snacks. Less than a week and Vito had the place clocked. From the constant cheers, Robert knew how this all played out. They all win a little one week, lose a little next week, win a little the following week, then at the end of the month the big score takes place. Praying his death angel would have a plan to get him out of here by then, Robert played along.

"You prick," Sal muttered, as the four of a kind killed the hand.

"What's the end game here boys?" Robert said, picking up the small stash of multi colored money in the middle of the table.

"Oh, it's a beauty. Every four weeks, we are looking at a cool dime a piece. Big man is thinking of branching out too. There are four other communities in the county," Tommy explained.

"Damn. It's just. These folks live on a set budget. Wouldn't want any of them to go without food or anything. Most of them already look like they haven't had a proper meal in a month," Robert said.

"Fuck them. Ain't no one holding a gun to their heads to play," Sal intervened.

"What if one goes to the office? Not supposed to be any gambling on site," Robert continued.

"Easy Bobby boy. Vito is cashing them in and out on the patio out back. No cameras out there. Anyone makes a stink, they won't again," Sal said, followed by a gagging laugh that was half laugh, half chock.

The game wound down as the white-haired crew waddled, limped, and strolled out of the media room. Some headed out back to get their winnings, some back to their rooms with a small loss.

Robert finished about a hundie up. He started counting out when two pudgy hands roughly started massaging his neck.

"You took them to the cleaners BABA BOOEY," Vito bellowed.

"I made out ok," Robert responded.

Vito squirmed into the small plastic chair next to him, opened his little notebook and started to write down numbers for the night. Tommy, Sal, and the other guy, Robert thought his name was Jay or James, had left a few minutes ago.

"Hey, we had to take a little loss tonight. I can cash you out next week. You know how the game goes," Vito said. His beady eyes examining the tiny notebook like it was a wall street ticker.

"Yeah, of course, no problem. Whatever works," Robert replied.

"Sal says you might take issue with game night?" Vito said, still not lifting his eyes from his pad. His fat hand grasping a slim pencil as he did elementary calculations.

"Nah, just don't want to see anyone take a bath that can't afford to," Robert replied.

"Have you smelled half of these people. I don't think some of them have had a bath in days," Vito responded. Whizzing out a laugh with his response, then he continued.

"Look, I ain't gonna clean anyone out, I got it all under control. Don't you worry bout nothing. And as for the staff, I got them covered. So, stop worrying so damn much, that was always your problem. Stop and smell the aftershave BABA BOOEY," Vito said, then excused himself to the patio where his fellow neighbors awaited their small payouts.

Robert knew how the game ended. It always ended like this for Vito and sadly some other poor sap. One of the residents would lose their social security checks. Their family would complain to the office. The office, on the payroll now, would ignore their complaint. It would get to corporate eventually. An office member would lose their job, Vito would get kicked out, then a senior citizen would catch a beating. The saga pissed Robert off, igniting another heat surge in his chest. Fresh off a feeding, I'm way more emotional he thought. Rounding the corner, a big angry orange tabby mugged the undead man. The damn place was filled with these things. Lonely old ladies would leave their doors open when visiting the neighbors or head out to the patio to gossip about the comings and goings at The Shores. This feline looked borderline rabid. It hissed, then exposed its very own set of sharp fangs at the vampire. Must sense what I am, like the dachshund did he thought. Robert slowly attempted to walk past the pussy. From its hind legs, a fur ball of orange leapt at him, digging deep into his thigh. Letting out a small grunt, Robert caught the tabby by its neck, with a twist of his wrist, the vampire snapped the neck of the cat with ease. A small crunch followed the twist. He held it up, met the cat's dead green eyes with his own now darkening pupils. Robert glanced both ways down the hall, then quickly headed to his door, cat in hand. Three steps into his apartment, he held the cat up again, this time for a late-night snack.

Chapter Eleven
October 11th

The taste of sweet butterscotch finally began to dissipate around early afternoon. Do all felines taste like this or just the tabby variety? Robert pondered that thought for a moment, then returned to the small map that shot back from his phone. Blinding ecstasy from his cat snack kept him up late. The kitty blood coursed sweetly through his undead body lighting up his entire being. After wrapping poor Garfield up in two trash bags, that was Robert's nickname for his dinner, he paced his living room with restless joy. Opening the patio several times to enjoy the moonlit night that carried heavy clouds through the darkness. His night eyes, fully fueled from his meal, watched rabbits scurry through the brush, owls swoop from branch to branch, and deer prance in formation in search for food. A few of the doe glanced once at him before quickly taking off into the dark night. Katie had mentioned their deliciousness before, Robert was looking forward to that hunt. Every time he tried to settle to watch a bit of television the night kept calling. Calling for him to bath in the darkness and track his treats. With every short trip outside, he would catch a glimpse of himself in the glass slider. A taunt sharp toothed monster with talons reflected back. The furry meal kept him in a transformed ecstatic state. Accompanying his visual acceleration was also that of the new gift of hearing. Soft footsteps from his neighbor above sounded like a herd of elephants stampeding through the desert. Jazz music playing from somewhere down the hall echoed into the apartment. Around dawn, silence along with mortal calm returned. Robert doubled up again on the trash, not wanting any hint of Garfield to be seen. He took the garbage out under the cover of a dark blue October morning sky. Once the sun said hello to the world, Robert was able to fall asleep with the sweet nectar of the cat tingling his gums. It was Monday and he had to plan his Sasha spy game. Coming to terms with the new found senses, Robert still needed some hard proof to take to his son. Matthew would think him mad if he presented him with just a hunch, knowing damn well that his father never accepted, nor took to his wife in the first place. Several motels ran adjacent to the large mall which offered temporary beds to mostly visiting business personnel that filtered in and out of the surrounding business park. It was also known as a part of town where hourly liaisons could be arranged at a reasonable rate. Robert drew his own amateur map mimicking the digital one he glared at in an attempt to narrow down his search. Satisfied with his plan, Robert closed out the map on his phone and dialed his son.

"Hey pop," Matthew gleefully spoke as he picked up the call.

"What's up buddy. Seeing what your crew is up to tonight. I might stop by," Robert questioned. Knowing full on well Sasha had plans and the boys were at soccer practice on Monday nights.

"Ahhh, the boys got practice and Sasha will be at the gym, then I think she is hanging with some of her girlfriends. Do you want to come watch the boys play?" Matthew said.

Robert was thrown off by the response. He had not thought about going to the boy's practice. Usually, he was only invited to games and usually when his grandkids were playing a soft opponent he always noticed.

"Ah shit. Um, lets shoot for another time. I just wanted to drop off something. I was going to be in and out, meeting up with a few of the old guys to play cards later," Robert replied, lying fast on his feet.

"More money? Just kidding dad. Man, we really appreciate the help pop. I want to talk to you about that, but we are flying around like crazy today. I have to leave for Toronto tomorrow for a conference, but when I get back you pick any spot for dinner just me and you pop," Matthew said.

"Canada huh? How long are you up there?" Robert questioned.

"About two weeks, single payer system conference. The good, the bad, and the expensive."

"You said it. Yeah buddy, call me when you get back. I'll pick the most expensive steak house in the city."

"You got it pop, talk to you then," Matthew said, then hung up.

Robert put his head in his hand in relief of his quick thinking to get out of that pinch. New anxieties began to form at his brow. Would he still be here when Matthew got back? Katie was due back in a week. Would he have to leave right away? Forget it he told himself. Regardless of what her plans were, Robert concluded that he would not leave until his son knew the truth. Until all scores were settled. Until all debts were paid.

Brisk autumn air circled through the car as Robert slowly drove past the gym entrance at the back of the mall. He parked far away from the front doors of the gym and gleamed with nocturnal vison through the ground to roof glass walls. Sasha was spot on with her assessment of the work-out facility. Men grunted and growled while throwing large weights methodically around. The vampire ears could hear their moans two hundred yards away through solid glass. The bulging veins in their necks beckoned for a nibble. Women trotted seductively on tread mills, pausing intermittently to take pictures of themselves with their phones. This was no place for a senior looking to keep fit. Robert let out a small laugh, thinking how they would react to seeing him dead lift a few hundred pounds. Night eyes continued the search for Sasha. From what he could put together she was to be allegedly at the gym from around eight to nine, then meeting mythical friends for drinks. Around eight thirty, Robert was convinced she was not here. Royal Inn was the first motel closet to the mall. Neon blue glared off of the entrance sign, shooting into Robert's eyes. He squinted, then seductively pulled his car around to the back parking lot. A spot of panic set in as he had wished he rented a car with tinted windows. What if she spotted him? Why was he feeling guilty when she was the one doing the deed? Questions sprung around him as Robert crept through the back looking for her gaudy white Mercedes. Nothing. Several minutes later the supernatural stalker pulled up to Seneca Suites. Nothing about the place said suites. The Royal Inn was a three-story decent looking humble place, the Seneca was a one-story wrap around lodge with the parking lot exposed in front. Quickly circling the small lot, Robert began to think she obviously was at her lover's house, not shacked up like two teens looking for a place to get their first taste. Five minutes later he drove past the glowing lights of the commercial town center. Robert made a left over cracked concreate which led to the entrance to The Wolves Den. The Den made the Seneca look like a Wyndham resort. Twenty rooms lined in a single-story row, stretched from the main road to a blacked-out forest. The forest was part of a state park, where a wicked flowing river ran up to the Pennsylvania line. He and Mary had gone tubbing on the water there many times in their youth. Distraught, strung-out, faces stared at Robert as he slowly made his way to the back of the complex. Each current resident wore the mask of desperation and fury, a smoke in one hand and cans of cheap beer in the other. A bearded fat man in too tight jeans and a black biker's vest stared with eager anger as Robert passed several bikes. He nearly came to a complete stop to avoid the slightest hint of bumping into any of them. Seeing an opportunity to turn around by the office area, he slowly turned to make a complete circle to flee from these denizens of despair. There it was. Gleaming white. Her car, hidden in the back lot, covered in the darkness of the overgrown oaks that cloaked the rear of the complex with cover. Justification and joy shot through Robert. He knew it dammit. Quickly the joy of being right was replaced with sadness and fury. Sad for his son, angry at this bitch. Glancing at the four other cars hidden in the back lot, he saw three modest trucks and a silver BMW. 5 Series. The obnoxious selection for most doctors. "Hey!" A skinny man shouted from his left. The man wore a tank top and was shoeless. He came from the office front door, approaching Robert's car quickly. Probably thinking the stalking senior was a cop or some older man looking for some young love. The Den was notorious for being a safe house for ladies of the night. Robert nodded, then pulled quickly toward to the exit. He could hear the deranged looking manager yelling and thought to stop and give him a glance at what real anger looked like, but choose a different route as he sped away from The Den. After parking the car at a nearby convenience store, Robert walked stealthily on the side of the road back toward the cheap motel. His night eyes blinded by the oncoming traffic, but he had plenty of space on the shoulder of the main road. The Den was about a hundred yards up on the left. Woods blanketed the entire area to the left of the road. Before he reached the motel, Robert snuck into the brush under cover of trees which were dressed in orange-colored leaves. He had to see her. Had to see who she was with. Before reaching the clearing to the motel there was a path that led from the hotel through the woods and down to the river. He could hear the water rushing north bound in the distance. Robert stopped short of the clearing, hidden by the deep dark foliage. Glancing right to left from the first room to the back office, he attempted to find which room the slut was in. Angry manager was dropping one slurred f bomb after another to fat biker man. Several of his buddies were outside now, smoking up a storm and spilling suds on their hairy faces. A few patrons came in and out of their rooms, mostly to have a smoke or sneak into another room to purchase more pick me ups. Relevant time was now obsolete to the newly formed immortal man, but the minutes felt like hours as Robert began to wonder how late she would stay out on her charade. The sound of woodland creatures interrupted his concentration and flared his temper. Here we go again he thought. Fingers twitched, gums numbing, Robert closed his eyes in attempt to calm down and focus. Her laugh broke his meditation. There she was! Sasha walked slowly, strolling, and laughing out of the first room by the office with a much older man following behind her. She was in workout clothes and looked sweaty, but not from hitting the bike of course. The man had to be at least sixty, at least forty pounds overweight, and he wore the permanent, red-stained, jolly face of a well feed wealthy medical professional. Robert worked with them for decades. As the two strutted to their cars, the patrons of the piss palace stared and smiled, taking mental pictures of Sasha's skinny toned ass. Her Mercedes flew out past him not twenty yards from where Robert was perched behind two bushes. Her lover's beamer followed. The creature of the night stepped forward to try and memorize the license plate but needed no mental fortitude to recall the tags. DRDBLD. The plates said it all. Plastic surgeon. Mary had mentioned after their second grandchild was born that Sasha wanted to get a boob job after breast feeding for the last time. Sadness filled his heart for Matthew. The kid deserved better. As scenarios on how he would break the news to Matthew fluttered through his thoughts, two things became crystal clear. He would make Sasha pay for this betrayal and he would make a personal house call to the good doctor in good time. Robert returned to the shoulder of the road, solemnly walking back toward his car. He heard the obscenity before it was completed. A teenage boy was yelling at the weirdo on the side of the road. The vampire turned and roared as the car flew past him, the teenager got a glimpse of the creature and sheltered from the horrific vision by jerking to his left. The frightened boy obviously hit his buddy driving, as the small two-seater swerved into the left lane, fortunately not hitting any other vehicle. Red lights signaled the two-seater coming to an abrupt halt. Robert waited. Night eyes saw the two young men shouting and looking back at the thing that was glaring at them through the passenger door mirror. Their quick consultation ended and burning rubber erupted on the pavement as the two scared little boys speed away from the demon. Robert forgot about Sasha for a brief moment. The undead man exposed a sharp toothed smiled.

Chapter Twelve
October 12th

Howling winds accompanied the drop in temperature as hints of the upcoming winter blew through Robert's close-cut hair. Typical Mid-Atlantic weather, frigid one day, humid the next. The cooling air felt good on his undead pale skin, helping to cool rampaging thoughts as well as heated emotions from the night before. Robert was a half hour early and expected to sit in his car listening to the morning news, but Dawn's truck was already parked in the front of the lot. To delighted surprise, Bruce's bike was chained in front of the store. Robert was eager to see his young buddy. See if his little talk with Kyle had done some good or hopefully get news that Bruce had left the degenerate. Debbie waddled quickly to the front entrance when she caught a glimpse of her co-worker approaching. She fumbled with the keys as Robert stood smiling outside. Finally getting the door to open, she stepped aside and shot glances back and forth into the deserted parking lot, then shut the door with force. Sealing the store as if someone were going to attempt to pull off a small stakes heist.

"Dawn needs to see you right away," Debbie stated, shaking her head up and down. Her flappy second chin following the serious vertical nod along with her skull.

"Okie Dokie," Robert replied.

He stole a giggle on his way to the office, Debbie's face told the story of something sinister that lurked in the land of cheap goods. What could be so dramatic as to cause this concern? Robert walked cautiously to the closed office door. He gave it three quick knocks to announce his arrival. The door crawled open, he saw Dawn sitting at her cheap metal desk, excel spreadsheets littered the top, accompanied by a supersized soda that sat half-drunk to her pudgy left arm. Bruce met his eyes before scurrying over to a file cabinet that stood behind Dawn.

"What's new good people?" Robert said, announcing his arrival. Dawn pointed to one of the two plastic chairs that sat in front of her desk. Robert strode over and sat, images of being called into a malpractice inquiry from his real working days scattered through his thoughts. Something was not right here.

"Bob. Did you go to Bruce's home the other day?" Dawn questioned. Her head pointed down as her swollen eyes shot up at her employee. Looking more like an inquisitive Franciscan from ancient France, than a simple store manager.

"Yeah, I wanted to check on him, like you said," Robert answered.

"I SAID NO SUCH THING!" Dawn yelped and continued.

"I said I would check on him when I got the chance. I am the manager Bob, not you. You had no right to go to his home and harass his friend."

Robert looked at Bruce, who stapled his eyes to the ground. "What in the hell is this Bruce? Buddy, I just came to see if you were sick or hurt, or in trouble. Kyle said you both had a fight, I just asked him where you might be?"

"I'm not your buddy, you freak," Bruce responded. Quickly raising his red stained eyes to Dawn before sprinting out of the office.

"What in the fuck?" Robert questioned to the air.

"Bob. Bruce said you went to his house and attacked his friend. Is that true?" Dawn asked.

"Look Dawn. I went to check on him, regardless if you said so or not. That friend has been laying his hands on the boy, I just scarred him a little," Robert responded.

"You know they are thinking of pressing charges?"

"Oh for fucks sake. Whatever, he wants to stay with that loser in that dump, fine. I won't get involved anymore," Robert explained. Trying to hold back a laugh at the thought of either of the two young boys taking enough initiative to file a proper charge against him.

"Either way I have to let you go. This is strictly against company policy," Dawn stated. She handed him a few pieces of freshly printed forms and continued.

"We also have to ban you from the store and all Dollar Land locations for up to one year. Like I said company policy."

Robert quickly glanced at the forms. He was embarrassed, upset, and angry. He had never been officially written up yet alone fired from any position he ever held.

Dawn broke his confused meditation, "I really expected a man of your age to use better judgement."

Old Robert would have thanked her for the opportunity, kindly excused himself, and wallowed in self-pity for a few days. New Robert had a different reaction.

"Ahhhhhh, you silly little woman. You think I give a flying fuck what you think of me? Have you looked in the mirror the last decade? I would say you look like a demented troll storming through this shitty store, but that would be demining to trolls. How long have you waisted your pathetic life here?"

Robert slowly tore the papers into tiny pieces and continued.

"I ban you. You arrogant asshole. I ban you from ever crossing paths with me again," Robert concluded. He stood and met Dawn's eyes. She trembled back in her chair; mouth open in disbelief. The kind and humble old man that she hired was replaced by a monstrous, strong, evil looking middle aged man. Robert blew her a kiss as he exited the office. He stole a quick glance to the back stockroom, where he could here Bruce attempting to whisper to someone on his phone. After two steps towards the whispers, he turned and made way to exit the store, feeling there was no use in berating the pathetic flesh puppet. The change began to tremble through him again. This time, he did not want to stop it. Several steps later he passed Debbie, who had her head down intensely glaring at a magazine. Ready to leave her, Dawn, Bruce, and the shithole behind he suddenly stopped. Debbie made a clucking noise out of her fat mouth, signaling her disapproval at Robert's shame.

"Excuse me?" Robert asked.

Dawn peered at him and started a retreat from the register to the back of the counter. Her back hit the shelves causing several packs of cigarettes to tumble to the floor.

"That's what I thought," Robert explained, then strutted out of the store. The reflection from the glass door showed him half turned, giving explanation to the quick backpedal from Debbie. The door was thankfully unlocked and the monster, not the man, left Dollar Land in his wicked wake.

Circling its prey for about an hour, the snake finally sprung and wrapped its elongated mouth around the mouse. The death dance nearly put Robert to sleep, but the finale sprung him back to life. He fully expected the snake to just jump its dinner at first sight. But the reptile was cunning. Would he be as clever as to stalk his victims with cunning? He thought not, the supernatural emotions were out of control. Stillness settled over the vampire after he returned home, but with stillness came reflection. No longer having to be anywhere at all until Katie came back, Robert seriously contemplated parking his ass on the sofa until her return. Confidence and rage felt good, but human emotions in the form of shameful regret still lingered. Regretting his attack on Kyle, snapping at the delivery guy and macho man at the bank. Shame at his verbal assault at the store. Thankfully, reason also returned to him. He had nearly full on turned several times and completely vamped out on Kyle. He must stay calm, must control his emotions, must wait for his maker to come back to him. Sasha. What of Sasha? Could he wait that out? Contemplation began to seep into madness and Robert did what he always did when his mind hoped along hopelessly without calm, he went for a nice long walk.

Thirty minutes after wandering aimlessly in the cold autumn night, the night creature found himself at the strip mall, which was about four miles from The Shores. Panic set in again. He thought his pace was that of a slow walk, but he covered way too much ground too fast. Looking back to the path he came from, a sense of relief washed over him. Most of the journey was through the parks and school lots that surrounded the area. Several shoppers gave him a strong once over as they passed him. Robert quickly turned to get a glimpse of himself in the sub shop window. Thankful that their awkward gazes were sent due to him still in his Dollar Land polo while most of the pedestrians had on heavy coats and beanie caps. The chilly evening felt terrific to the undead man, but the mortals were shivering as the unexpected early wintry blast hit their fragile skin. Robert passed the sub shop and other small eateries before deciding to take a stroll through the discounted grocery store. Not dismayed by his lack of taste anymore, he still craved some fresh fruit to nibble, thinking the appearance of having food in the house would be good to ward off any suspicious visitors. Especially if Matthew stopped over and saw no food in the fridge. But Matthew was north of the border right now. The thought that no one else was stopping by brought back anxieties. The quick return of dismay was replaced with a bout of excitement. Why care anymore? What is done is done. It has been one hell of a ride and dark circumstance would give him eternal opportunities to start over, start over, and start over again. He played it safe his entire mortal life, where had that gotten him? Walking alone down the snack aisle as obese creatures contemplated the purchase of popcorn and pretzels. Night by night, Robert started to loath the mortal world as he begin to embrace the night life. Sea smells fluttered around his nose, signaling the fresh seafood counter. Raw fish lay in perfect formation, their dead eyes staring blankly out of their iced tomb. Would he be able to enjoy some raw fish or the area's famous crab? A frown froze on his face, thinking that he might never enjoy the flavor of a hot crab cake with mustard again. Turning away he also remembered with hope, Katie talking about the ecstasy of animal blood and his thoughts turned to the tiny taste of the dancer as well as the exotic draining of the kitty. With lack of any true hunger rumbling, Robert exited the store, ready to make the trek home. Prepared to be more cautious of his speedy movements this time. As in his mortal life, the walk did him good. Dollar Land, Sasha, all of his worries were stamped away with the scattering of his sneakers.

"Excuse me sir," A young woman said. She appeared to be in her early twenties and was hanging seductively against the Red Box that sat at the end of the shopping center.

"Yes," Robert replied.

"Do you have any spare change? I left my money at home and walked in the cold to get some milk for my baby." The woman explained.

Robert dug in his pocket, quickly pulling out a small wad of cash. He peeled off a five and handed it her. He caught her excited expression upon seeing the small stack which added up close to a hundred.

"Do you think I could get a twenty. Maybe we could work something out?" she asked.

Old Robert would have just given her the twenty, always counting his economic blessings and empathizing for the disadvantaged. New Robert reacted differently.

"A gallon in there is about three dollars, keep the change, ya hear," Robert responded, then walked away from the temptress.

"Dick, I didn't ask how muc..." The woman began as she went to give Robert a shove to his shoulder.

The vampire's quick unnatural instincts sensed the incoming blow and the creature responded by turning at a lightning pace, slapping the beggar in unison with the turn, sending her flailing into the red movie machine. The loud thump would have made his heart skip a beat if it still beat. He thought her head had snapped at impact. Vile words spewed from her mouth as she tossed around on the concrete floor, both hands rubbing her injured temple. Quickly and thankfully realizing she was just going to have one hell of a headache, Robert turned and put his new supernatural speed to the test. Seconds later only a faint glow from the center shone in the distance. He felt the safety in the darkness of the empty park blanket him.

Chapter Thirteen
October 13th

Murky black shadows fell through the bedroom like silent thieves in the night. The darkness that crept through the blinds announced early evening. A quick glance at his phone upon awakening showed eight PM. Robert nearly fell out of his humble queen-sized bed. Always one to be up and at it, the shock of the time sent cold shivers through his spine. Quickly replaying the last twenty-four hours. The shitshow at the store. The near decapitation of the beggar. He remembered jogging back to the park area after fleeing to see if she was o.k. from a distance. She was more than fine and still hustling for the mythical milk money. What then, it was television and off to bed. Grabbing his phone, he tried to make sense of the long slumber. More than a dozen text alerts stood unread at the top of his cell. A final recollection was that of walking to bed around the start of the morning news. He chalked it up to the exhaustion of the last couple days and his newly formed internal clock, which he figured held sway to the moon instead of the sun now. Sitting on the side of the bed, Robert opened his text application and flipped through the messages. Five from Vito, four each from Tommy and Sal. All of them telling him to get his old ass to Vito's tonight for some fun. The last few asking where the hell he was at? Robert's night ears picked up a soft shuffle approaching his front door, on command a soft rattle followed. Twenty steps later, Tommy greeted him at his entrance.

"Hey Bobby boy, where the hell you been all day?" Tommy questioned.

Letting out a yawn, Robert replied, "Long night yesterday, I could not get to damn sleep. Damn heart pills got me all wired," He threw in the antidote for good measure.

"Well get your tired old ass together, we got some fun stuff over at Vito's spot."

"Next time brother, I got to get back to bed, try and get some rest."

"Sleep when you die Bobby boy, an old friend is waiting for you over there. You are not going to want to miss this. Trust me," Tommy explained.

At internet speed, Robert played out the scenario. Sit up all night and worry away or have a few drinks with the boys. Besides his dismay at Vito taking the seniors for a ride at card night, he actually had been enjoying the few outings with the old gang.

"Sure, Sure, just let me get myself together," Robert said.

"There ya go Bobby boy, and shower and change man, you look like death on a cracker," Tommy said, turning and taking off toward Vito's apartment with too much energy for a sickly old man.

Death on a cracker? Tommy, you nailed it. The weary vampire headed to the bathroom to give himself a once over. Still adorning his Dollar Land polo and khaki pants, Robert took a good whiff of himself. Not only did he look like death, but he smelt it as well. Cool water sprouted from the shower head. The icy feeling rejuvenated the cold-blooded creature beneath the cascade. After a good long soak and wash, Robert wiped the fog from the mirror. A confident, good looking, strong man of about fifty stared back. He looked good, he smelled good, he felt great.

Soft rock poured from Vito's place, a guitar chord rattled through the hall, it did not take mystical hearing to know that it was being played entirely too loud. The door was slightly ajar as Robert strolled in, decked out in a comfy sports sweatshirt and jeans, expecting to just be having a few drinks with the boys. A carnival of booze, girls, and drugs greeted him. Vito had a two bedroom and den. The living room was much bigger than Robert's and was engulfed by an enormous H-Shaped sofa. Sal sat in the middle of the massive cotton couch. Two women hung on each side of him, Tommy stood by the sliding door with another woman. Robert recognized the ladies from the club.

"Bobby!" Sal and Tommy shouted once they took notice of his arrival.

Robert smiled as he headed over to the living room.

"Hey stud," A female voice whispered to his right.

Vito's kitchen was also larger than his own galley style. The layout was circular. A faux granite table housed two chairs on the side across from the appliances. Luna sat at the chair farthest away. Her cheap perfume danced from her neck, waltzing into Robert's nose, filling him with desire. He slowly strode over to the empty chair and sat.

"And how are we doing tonight pretty lady?" he questioned.

A giggle escaped her lips, "Great, really great. I'm glad you could make it."

"What the hell is going on here?" Robert asked.

"Big boy hit the machine big time. He rounded us up today for a little after work party." Luna responded. She took a small plastic shot cup and poured cheap tequila into it. Sliding it over to Robert after the yellow liquid hit the brim. The strong smell of mescal overtook the perfume. Luna's bloodshot eyes had Robert putting her shot count into double digits.

"Grassy Ass," he said, quickly downing the shot with only a slight sensation of heat hitting his numb tongue. Luna burst into laughter at his Hispanic play on words.

"Where is big boy anyway?" Robert asked.

"Skiing in his room with Tiffany," Luna answered. Robert's inquisitive look made her explain.

"She loves the nose candy. Coke. Cocaine Bobby."

Robert nodded in acknowledgement and asked if there was any beer as Luna started to pour two more shots. She pointed to the fridge with one hand as she poured with the other. Cheap domestic cans filled the bottom shelf, Robert took one and turned to investigate the living room. Tommy and the rail thin woman walked past the sofa into the den that sat off of the room. Two twigs about to get intertwined. Sal and one of the women on the sofa were leaned back, heads tilted forward, with soft moans exiting from their mouths. Robert's sharp eyes spotted the pills spread in unison at the end of the table. The other woman, legs hoping and shoulders shaking, was typing on her phone like a courtroom stenographer.

"Man, they are tuning out early," Robert said. He reclaimed his seat, beer in hand. His shot greeting him at the end of the table.

"Bobby, we've been here for two hours. All waiting for you. Well, I've been waiting for you," Luna said. Lifting her shot in salute then launching it down her throat. Robert mimicked her as he took shot number two. Popped the lid of the beer and took a small sip.

"So, how far to your place?" Luna asked.

"I'm right up the hall," Robert answered.

"I'd love to see it," Luna said.

Robert took a long drink to break up the inevitable scenario. The last time he took anyone to his bed besides Mary, was well over forty-seven years ago. Would he be able to even do it? Would he be able to control himself during the throws of passion? If he turned, would she freak the fuck out? Lowering his beer, a few signals helped him make the decision. Luna's head softly nodded side to side, clearly in the nearly passed out stage of inebriation. As she rocked forward, the tops of her brilliant breast crept out from her cheap black low-cut sweater. He was not going to pass this up. Even if it went sideways, the cunning creature was confident he could quickly clean up any mess and get her back to Vito's. If she had a long-toothed tale to tell, who would believe her in this state.

"Sure, follow me to my humble abode pretty lady," Robert said.

"Yeaaaahhh Bobby," Luna slurred, grabbing the half empty bottle to accompany her on the short journey.

Luna staggered down the fluorescent lite hallway humming some tune she heard earlier in the evening. The bottle swayed in unison with her luscious round ass. Black jeans fell from her hip revealing another half crescent blue moon tattoo on the small of her back. Robert accelerated past her at dizzying speed, he unlocked the door as Luna kept on walking past their desired destination.

"Hey lady, we have arrived," Robert said. Luna turned and laughed as he gestured her forward. She stepped past him with a gleam in her big brown eyes. As soon as Robert closed the door behind him, Luna wrapped her arms around him and planted her thick lips on his. The sensation caused an immediate heat to pulse through him. She quickly turned into the kitchen as the automated lights came on. Tilting the bottle to her lips, the seductive woman nearly inhaled the remnants of the bottle. Robert was grateful. She would be nearly passed out in no time.

"Which way to the bedroom daddy?" Luna asked.

Briefly shamed with the daddy wording, Robert smiled and waved her toward the bedroom. He turned at the edge of his bed and watched his drunken lover stumble in. She put the near empty bottle on his dresser, then tore off her clothes. Robert slowly undressed as he watched. Topless, Luna struggled to get her pants off and tumbled once laughing as she tripped over one pant leg. Robert helped her up.

Their eyes met. Cole black and wooded brown. The vampire tilted her head to the side and whispered,

"It's been a long time Luna. I haven't been with anyone but my late wife in decades."

A hint of sadness joined lust in her eyes as she responded, "No worries Bobby, I'll take over from here."

Good to her word, Luna did all the work. After escaping her silk panties, she dropped to her knees and took Robert into her mouth. Feasting on his flesh with rigorous fervor. Robert closed his eyes as the change shuttered through him. His cock bulged as the excess blood poured to the hot spot. Clawed hands grasped her midnight hair as he enjoyed the steady movement of her mouth. Luna stood and attempted to push her lover onto the bed. The first shove did not cause a flinch. Robert recognized the motion and fell backwards on his own accord with her second attempt. Luna pounced on his pulsating dick, her soaking wet woman cave capturing him. Her screams of ecstasy shattering his eardrums as she climaxed over and over and over again for a good half an hour. Robert fixated on her perfect tits bouncing in perfect harmony with her gait. After the initial transformation, a wave of calm ecstasy stilled the beast inside. His fangs had sprouted, his nails extended, his eyes narrowed and darkened but all was hidden in the pitch darkness of the room. Luna's insides felt like velvet joy as he enjoyed the ride. After what had to be her tenth orgasm, Luna finally faded and dismounted her dark stallion. Legs quivering and out of breath she laid in complete exotic elation. Only a few moments passed before Luna went out like a light. Before closing her eyes for the night, she turned sideways towards Robert. Her left breast hung perfectly over her crunched up right. A small blue vein ran from the top of her pointed nipple towards her shoulder. The sight of the blue against her milky white skin called to him. With each labored exhausted breath, the breast would swell and slightly deflate giving the illusion of a beacon calling for his bite. Getting rode like a wild boar was amazing but the eager anticipation of the bite made something wet dribble from Roberts still erect dick. Did he just cum? Glancing down, several crimson specks hung to the hair on his inner thigh. Robert laid flat, closed his eyes, desperately attempting to calm his physical and mental state. Something inside him pulled his eyes open, urging him to turn toward her. Something that was not Robert at all. The undead man leaned forward and took Luna's large breast into his mouth, more liquid shot from his cock. Upon opening his sharp toothed mouth wider, he punctured her skin softly, hitting paydirt. Luna's blood seeped into his mouth, crawled down his tongue and into his eager throat. Every pure emotion of bliss sprinted though his supernatural body. Recognition and reason fell over him as Luna appeared to awaken from the strong sucking. Robert pulled away. His lips drenched in rose colored ruin. Once again lying flat with eyes shut, he allowed the life liquid to invigorate his undead spirit.

Chapter Fourteen
October 14th

Drizzle pelted the top of his cotton hat as Robert twirled the ball in his glove, contemplating the next pitch. The proud pitcher always felt immortal on the mound, standing tall above his opponent, ready to fire the leather sphere with fury or cunning deceit. A large Texan crowded the plate. How he hated the players from the south. They reeked of arrogance and cavalier. Always attempting to impose intimidation at every turn instead of relying on skillful tactic. How he hated throwing in the rain as well. Robert's commanding control put to the test by tears from the heavens. A quick signal from the catcher and he turned, firing a dart to first, nearly nicking the sleepy runner. His teammate slapped his glove viciously against the diving opponent's wrist, causing the first base coach to erupt in a fit of fury. Shouts from both black outed dugouts rang through the rain. Angry blank faces full of fire. Big blue behind the plate shouted warnings to both teams as the light drizzle turned to steady rain. One more out. This was it. This is what he was born to do. Bottom of the ninth, up one, two outs. Just sit this lone star loser down and it would probably be enough to punch his ticket to the show. Turned sideways, he got the signal. The call was to brush big boy back, Robert nodded in agreement. A bit dangerous if the pitch got away from him, the prick on first could get in on a single at that point, but better to get the monster at the plate to step back a bit instead of taking him yard and blowing the lead. Robert brought his glove and ball bearing hand together, shooting a quick death glare at the batter. Rose colored rain dripped from the brow of his cap, his concentration not allowing him to see the blood droplets pour down from above. The Texan gave a big-league spit as he hovered even further over the plate. Robert reared back and threw with the might of a deity. As the lace left his hand, he instantly knew he went too far inside too fast. As predicted, the ball ran fast, clocking the batter's covered temple before he could duck out of the way. The echo of the ball hitting the helmet shattered the sky and was accompanied by a cracking thunder in the distance. Everyone on the field, in the dugouts, and in the stands appeared to vanish as the Texan turned in anger toward Robert. He had seen that look before. In quick response, he tossed his mitt quickly in anticipation of the charge. The impact of the ball cut the Texan, Robert could make out the incision as the batter tossed his helmet and sprinted toward his assailant. The batter grew bigger as he got closer. Robert sent a quick prayer for one of his teammates to intercept the beast before he got to him. None arrived to assist. Five steps away and charging through a curtain of blood rain, the sight of the enormous figure should have caused Robert to retreat. Instead, his mouth opened, accompanied by a hideous hiss. His fangs shot out, his mortal hands became taloned weapons. Robert sidestepped the initial right cross and grabbed the Texan by his shoulder blades. A quick head butt crushed the batter's nose. The trickled blood from his temple met the streaming red flow from his nose. Robert placed his tongue on the batter's chin and took a deep long lick. Digging his left hand into the right side of the Texan's cheek, Robert tilted the massive young man's head backwards then bit deep into his thick neck. The Texan gurgled vulgarity as Robert sucked his life away. Power and strength poured out of one player into another. The taste of an athlete in his prime was extraordinarily exquisite. The Texan fell limp after a minute. Robert tossed the bloodless sack over his left shoulder. Blood drunk, the vampire, decked in red stained pinstripes, let out a horrific roar that shook the metal bleachers throughout the stadium.

Beams of heat snuck through the blinds and danced on the sleeping monster's face, rousing him awake. He had taken at least a half glass full of blood from his lover's breast during their flesh tango. The ecstasy still coursed through his body. Luna was star shaped spread next to him, still lying in an alcohol induced nude deep sleep. Robert mimicked a deep exhale, but no breath accompanied the display. Reaching with his right arm, he fumbled for his phone. Seven AM glared back at him. He gently tossed the phone back on the side table then took a quick recount of the night. A smile broke out across his face, the sex was phenomenal, the dream that followed was equally exquisite, the taste of her tit was exhilarating. A quick glance to his left told another tale. A steady trail of blood ran from Luna's left breast, across her chest and sat in a tiny puddle between them. Another glance downward revealed blotches of blood caked to Robert's inner left thigh, with a red wet line running to his cock. Robert flew off the side of the bed and towered over his lover to assess the damage. In a vampiric flash, the night creature shot into the bathroom. Quickly washing off the red stains with freezing water and peroxide from the sink. Manually scrubbing without the assistance of the power of the shower, not wanting the sound of steady water to cause his guest to awaken in a blood bath. Satisfied with his personal quick fix, still nude, he went to work cautiously on Luna and the sheets. Her stocky body moving easily under his newly found strength. She stirred a few times but did not come close to rising from her slumber. Using peroxide and his scented body wash, Robert gently removed the hardened blood that speckled her nude front. Skills from his mortal profession helped to make for a quick clean up. With most of her body clear he reached the source of the wound. Her large left breast hung to the left of her frame, nearly all covered in blackish red blood. He gently massaged his concoction in a circular motion, quickly clearing up patches inch by inch and causing her nipple to harden. The alluring touch of her breast causing him to start to harden again as well. The entire breast was nearly cleared. Robert was about to head back to the bathroom to get one final towel to remove the small spots left when he noticed a much bigger problem. Two inches above her perfect pink nipple sat two perfect puncture marks that appeared to run at least an inch deep. The wound was the darkest shade of red he had ever seen. The vampire closed his eyes tightly for a quick consultation. One thing at a time he repeated to himself. Robert sprang back into action. Tossing the blood-soaked towels into the hamper, he found a pair of sweats to put on. After dousing a small rag full of peroxide and ocean scented body wash, he returned to his patient with plan in place. First, the former nurse took the sheets from under the mattress then folded them over the stained portion next to Luna. Picking up the small rag he hovered over the dark beauty, he softly wiped the last remnants clean. Gritting his teeth, Robert turned the rag over and tried to wipe the small scabs clear of wound entry. The desired effect took place as the hardened tops of the scabs sizzled, then cleared up. Two tiny holes appeared, then slowly began to fill with refreshed pinkish blood. Lips quivering again, Robert closed his eyes with steel reserve, attempting to drive away the calling. Picturing himself back in the ER with a patient's life on the line. The mental exercise worked. Calm and focused, he contemplated what the best course of explanation would be when Luna would wake. You told me to bite you? You dug your nails into yourself? Robert convinced himself that this lady of the night had seen worse, plus the cleaned wound looked perfectly able to heal without permanent scarring. Satisfied and relived, Robert pushed all of the red stained clothes to the bottom of his hamper, pulling the older occupants over top of the evidence. Now wanting to wake her and send Luna on her way, he stripped out of his comfy sweats, got in the shower, and made as much racket as he could while washing up. Steady cranking the cold knob to full blast, the frigid water calmed the frightened fanged man. Serenity flowed over his undead skin. His strong hands felt like they would go through the ceramic tile as he held himself upward to relax. Another frighting thought appeared. Did he just turn her? What had Katie said? It would take liters of blood to turn someone. But he turned quick due to his age? How old was Luna? Thirty? Thirty-five? Robert hung his head while letting out a disgruntled moan. When the fuck was Katie due back? Two days? Three days? Stirring from the bedroom interrupted his silent tirade. Robert shut off the shower, wrapped a towel around his newly fit form and put on his best good morning demeanor.

"Good morning moonshine," Robert said. Luna sat hunched, running her hands through her strangely hair. Robert noticed with enhanced vision; a few red specks tangled in her black locks.

"Hey," Luna replied. Her voice hoarse from alcohol.

"You want some water and Tylenol?" Robert questioned.

"That would be great, thanks," Luna answered.

Luna stood and made way toward the bathroom. Robert started to head to the kitchen when he felt her warm arms wrap around him. Her bare breast pressed firmly against his strong back. She kissed the back of his neck once then stumbled into the bathroom. A few minutes later she appeared in the hallway and made way to the kitchen. Her wrinkled clothes clumsily thrown over her ravaged body. Robert walked a large glass of ice water over to her. Luna took the water and the two Tylenol he also offered. She inhaled the drink, swallowed the pills, then headed over to the kitchen sink to refill her glass.

"You tore me up last night Bobby boy. I haven't felt this sore downstairs since my first time," She said.

"Jeez, well it's been a long time since I've been with a woman. Guess I had a lot of built-up energy," Robert responded.

Giggling, Luna continued, "Well, I can make sure you don't have to wait too long between romps anymore."

Rounding the kitchen corner, she strolled up to Robert with lust crusted in her eye, she spoke again,

"And I don't want any money this time. I really dig you."

"Wow, thank you. But I'm sure you have plenty of lovers more your age," Robert said.

"They aren't packing what you are Bobby boy," Luna said. She wrapped her left hand around his neck, her right hand gave his junk a tug, her tequila flavored lips wrapped against Robert's thin chilly mouth.

"Shit, did I bring my pocketbook here last night?" she questioned after the kiss.

"Nah, I think you left it at Vito's," Robert answered.

"Ugh, that fat pig is disgusting. How do you put up with him?" Luna said, looking around for something. She found it, then headed over to the dry erase board on the fridge.

"I try not to," Robert explained.

Luna used her bare hand to wipe off some scribbled note as she put her name and number on the board, drawling a small heart underneath the numbers.

"I got to get my kid to school. Call me please, O.K.?" Luna asked.

"Of course I will," Robert answered.

The two shared one last peck before Luna fluttered out of the apartment like a bird with a broken wing. Robert could have really gone without knowing she was mother to a child. Cold water ran from the sink upon his command, holding his hands under the water and periodically splashing some on his face helped him focus. Refreshed and feeling strong he opened the fridge and took out a beer. His ass slid comfortably into the indentation of his favorite spot on the sofa. Smiling while sipping the flat ale, Robert reflected again. After Mary died, the thought of being with another woman had never crossed his mind, yet alone making love to one. Making love? That was the furthest thing to describe what happened last night. The afterglow of the encounter quickly dissipated as thoughts returned to Mary. What on earth would she think of him. The sex, the violent outburst, the thing he was slowly becoming. For Christ's sake he thought, he could have drained Luna dead dry. And the dreams. Mary baking a blood pie, tearing the Texan apart. What was all of this? Once again, how the fuck could Katie leave him like this? Same as Mary, she had to think better of him than this. Their Robert would never indulge in this kind of behavior. Their Robert would never strike a woman. Their Robert would never use a dark gift to take a woman to bed. After effects from his dark drink stole over reason. Well, Mary was not here, was she? She was stolen from him. And Katie. Katie abandoned him. Katie created this nocturnal nightmare that grew stronger and darker with each passing night. Robert had renewed fortitude from his quick tit shot from Luna, but the morning sun still made him drowsy. Small beams peeked through the sliding door blinds and heated his exposed feet. The sun touch begging him to rest. Robert sat his beer down on the table and laid horizontally on the sofa, ready for another lengthy day nap.

Chapter Fifteen
October 15th

Long bombs and diving catches were playing rapidly on the nightly highlight show. A peaceful day of watching sports interrupted by the commotion outside. The west coast game, a twelve-inning thriller, ended after midnight and Robert wondered who the hell was whispering loudly outside of his door. Praying that Vito's crew was sleeping off the previous night's party so not to have to replay his romp to them. Robert spit a small strip of raw turkey bacon into his hand and placed it on a napkin that sat between five empty beer cans. The mild flavor brought forth a fangless smiled surprised, after trying several food concoctions the new vampire discovered that the raw pork product actual still held a hint of taste. Nearly devouring an entire pack during the epic ball game caused some stomach swelling, but the bite was worth the bloat. Hints of Luna's drink lingered through him all day. At first expecting to be wired to the hilt, his medical conclusion was that most of his quick tit sip was shot out down below during his vampiric orgasm. Two soft knocks came from the other side of the front door before he could peer out of the peep hole to see what was going on in the hallway. A quick glance through the small hole announced the arrival of Tommy. Robert unlocked the door to greet his old acquaintance.

"Hey Tommy, what's going on?" Robert whispered, with the door only slightly opened. Four other female residents of The Shores were speaking in low tones to Tommy's right, all of them with tear-stained reddened eyes.

"Missus Blankenship is checking out," Tommy replied.

Robert saw Tommy take a step forward, in response he opened the door fully to let him in. The four grieving ladies all shot disapproving looks at the two men. Noticing their company or commiseration was not wanted, Robert closed the door quickly behind his buddy.

"Who is Missus Blankenship?" Robert started.

"Your neighbor. One of the old guard of this place. Part of the crew that's huddled outside. She's been out of it for a few weeks, waiting in line at heaven's door. Been there myself," Tommy explained.

"Damn, sorry to hear that."

"Don't be. She was a real pisser. Like the rest of those bitchy bag ladies out there. All they do is hang in the lobby and talk shit all day. They already ran to the office about Vito, but he has the staff on the payroll."

"Until I knew you guys were here, I hardly paid anyone any mind."

"Yeah, they are a real can of worms. I was heading back from Vito's and saw them all in the hall, I just wanted to check in on ya and see how last night went?" Tommy questioned. An ear-to-ear grin popping up on his pallet.

Robert gave a wry smile as he explained. "Man, she passed out right after we got back here. Damn shame, It's been a long time since I've been with a woman. How did you guys all make out?"

"Vito got into it with his girl and Sal was out like a light before he could do anything. The big man said Brooke tried to lift one of his watches or some shit like that. What the hell would they do with a twenty-dollar thrift store watch?" Tommy stated. Spitting out a laugh and late-night cough with his replay of the previous night's events.

The voices got louder in the hall as Tommy propped open the door to check the news. A young priest arrived. Joyously welcomed by the gaggle of old ladies, all of them eagerly waiting for the holy man to forgive Missus Blankenship for all her sins before sending her to the lord.

"Welp, the taxi cab to the clouds just arrived," Tommy explained.

Robert fought back a laugh, "That's cleaver, you got a million of them."

"You fight off the man in black as many times as I have, you learn them all. Looks like they are heading in the room. Good time to make my escape. See ya at the game Sunday Bobby boy," Tommy finished.

Robert walked with him into the hallway and saw Tommy disappear towards his one-bedroom unit. Cheap body lotion and hairspray fluttered through the long corridor, but Robert picked up a strong sweet and sour smell that excited and scared him all the same. It was the alluring aroma of blood and death.

Pressing a nocturnal ear flat against the bedroom wall, the young priest could be heard giving last rights. The ladies whispering lies under fake tears and the shuffling of swollen feet exiting his dying neighbor's apartment echoed through the thin drywall. Creeping to the front door as if under supernatural surveillance, the eager vampire listened in to the arrangements. Missus Blankenship would not last the night. Her son was on his way from Philadelphia to take care of business upon arrival. The priest asked the women to take turns staying with her until she took her trip up the golden elevator. They all agreed. Once convinced the priest had left, not a one of them stayed. Robert was not shocked at all. A few weeks after Mary passed, his phone sat silent except for calls from his son and there were no more knocks at his door. The selfish nature of human beings had Robert subconsciously happy to now think of them as food. Food. Drink. No hunger rattled in his throat, no thirst lingered in his mouth, but the whiff of blood from the hallway tugged at his undead desires. After slowly steeping out of his apartment, Robert glanced both ways down the hall and crept toward Missus Blankenship's final home. What was left of his human heart begged for the door to be locked, his vampiric wanting was happy to discover that it was not. The allure of the drink resonated. Two incisors slowly grew into fangs. Ten fingernails shot into talons. Labored breath drew him into the old lady's bedroom at the end of a stain carpeted hallway. Wooden frames held the history of the dying woman, the photos shot disapproving glares at the monster who was now stalking her. Fifty pounds over healthy weight, but still looking frail, the dying woman laid helpless before the beast. A five-inch gap between Missus Blankenship's heavy socks and the bottom of her medical dress exposed red purplish marbling. The thirst was taking hold, but Robert had seen this skin tone a thousand times before, a physical phone call to the angle of death. He lifted his head and turned back towards the hallway, listening to see if anyone would interrupt his late-night drink. Only silence and the steady hum of an electric heater made any noise. In response, the vampire began sniffing vigorously as the essence of her dying skin filled the room. Tommy was right, she smelled rotten, full of hate and misery, loathing, and despair. This woman did not live any semblance of a clean, proper life, which was probably why she lay alone in her final hour. After a brief internal consultation, Robert slipped the top of her sock from mid-shin to her swollen ankle on her right leg. Spider webbed veins exploded through the usually covered pale white skin. Robert grasped her fat ankle with one clawed hand and her bloated thigh with the other as he chomped down on a juicy calf. Carefully slurping with the same control as he did with Luna's breast, letting dying burgundy blood pour into his lower lip. A few seconds past before withdrawing his bite. Two perfect holes quickly coagulated and blackish fluid slowly began to pour from the wound. Quickly pulling her thick sock up, Robert gave the now dead woman a once over, then, with supernatural speed, flew out of the deceased den and back to the safety of his secure sofa. Eyes closed and mouth still holding the liquid remains of his snack, Robert embraced the ecstasy.

As every different brand of beer delivered a different taste, so too did humans, the new creature of the night discovered. Luna's life liquid was sweet, full, and tasted like sex on a stick. Missus Blankenship's blood was bitter, filled with rage, like a bad artichoke eaten before full bloom. Whatever the flavor of flesh from the jump, the after effects were delectable. Robert's senses were at full peak, his strength making him feel like an invincible giant. The sensual tingling that flowed through him was like getting an internal deep tissue massage. Once more, rumblings murmured outside of his door. A few men spoke in low empathic tones. Robert quickly deduced that it was Missus Blankenship's son and a few EMT'S moving in to collect the corpse. A quick human anxiety fit took place. What would they make of her wounded calf? Would there be an investigation? Reason took over. Robert knew they would hardly give the wound a second glance. This was an old sick woman and he had been to many morgues. They will cut, fill, dress up and release, like an unwanted catch from the sea. By the time dawn arrived, the blood buzz wore off and Robert was ready for another day nap. Thinking more mortally now, he planned out his weekend. Katie would be back soon and after her rant about not drinking any human blood, he felt the need to stay imprisoned in his own home. Both he and his slithering pet were well fed. His taste of the tit and swollen limp leg had awoken some yearning. It was way too dangerous to venture out anymore. Robert wisely decided to fill the weekend with ballgames. He had a sudden urge to watch as many vampire films as he could. Flipping through a small notebook, the words Sasha sat below Monday the 18th of October. Matthew was away. Was her weekly workout always on Monday's? Should he risk confronting her? Should he just take some photos to back up the tale he would tell his son? Scribbled under Sasha's name was Katie as well. Katie should be back by Monday. Should he wait for her counsel? Would she tell him not to concern himself with mortal problems anymore? As alluring as immortality was, Robert knew he had to make sure his son and grandkids were fine before willingly embarking on this life in the night.

Chapter Sixteen
October 16th

Crisp autumn air crawled in through the opened sliding glass door. Robert cracked it open yesterday as he started his fang fest movie marathon, impressing himself by using the voice control on his remote. By simply saying, "Vampire movies," hundreds of options burst upon the flat screen. The two Corey's battled punk rocker vamps, James Woods lead a team of hard-core hunters, and he was currently into the fourth film of a series where vampires were battling werewolves. Wait, Lycans, yes that was what the clever team behind these films called them. Traveling and feeding on high end animals sounded fairly fun when Katie pitched the night life to him, but the twenty-four-hour mindless entertainment marathon had Robert wondering if sitting on a sofa and just chilling out for all of eternity would not be a better choice. Since he nearly broke every rule that Katie had laid out for him in less than a week, the thought of being a good boy for decades seemed impossible. Especially with how the calling of blood had seduced him the previous night. Relieved to not have any calls or knocks at the door, Robert was confident he had escaped any repercussions. Kyle, the staff at Dollar Land, Luna, and Missus Blankenship all sunken memories without any shrapnel to show for. End credits rolled into a small space on the screen and a list of new options popped up. Thinking his vampiric eyes deceiving him, Robert had to lean his head forward to glare at the title of the next film in line to make sure he was not going mad. Did that say Abraham Lincoln Vampire Hunter? Strong rapid knocks on the door interrupted his fit of laughter. Sure as shit, the serenity would not be eternal, Robert thought as he slowly walked to the front door. Surprised that no cramping crawled through his legs that had been at sitting position for several hours, but not completely surprised, his personal blood bank was full by all account. Half of Sal's fat head engulfed the vision beyond the small glass slit.

"Aye Bob, whatcha up to?" Sal said, as he walked through the open door, past his host, frantically looking into the living room, not wanting to meet Robert's eyes.

"Just watching some horror stuff, it being October and all," Robert replied.

"Yeah, so was I earlier. Dumb shit about a girl that comes through the TV or something. Who thinks up this shit? Any who, Vito would like to talk to ya," Sal said.

"Sure, where is he?"

"Outside the lobby, having a smoke. The dumb asshole already set off the sprinkler in his place trying to be slick."

"Jeez, they are strict with that stuff here. Let me put on some shoes and I'll meet you guys out there."

"Nah, just him, I got a thing in town. But I'll catch up with ya at the game tomorrow," Sal replied, then hustled out the door, still never meeting Robert's face square.

After the door slammed shut, the questions came like a tsunami of annoyance. What did this idiot want now? Why couldn't he finish his smoke and come over after? The heat began to surge again with his pulsating annoyance, this time in his throat instead of his chest. A perfect cut appeared on one of his laces, as his now protruded thumb nail sliced the string as he tried to pull it into a neat bow. Eyes closed and head back, Robert let the cool wind from outside hit his skin as he envisioned Katie sitting by his side. Any day now. The mental exercise worked. Normal human hands reappeared instantly, he was starting to get this thing under control. In green neon, nine PM shot out from the microwave, Robert hoped to be back by nine-fifteen.

"BABA BOOEY! Over here buddy." Vito yelled. He was at the far corner of the parking lot, a fat cigar cradled in his fat hand. Robert waived and slowly walked toward him. The light of the moon and crisp October breeze tremendously trembled through his eyes, lighting up the nocturnal beast dressed in man flesh.

"Hey Vito, what's going on?" Robert asked, both hands in his windbreaker to give the illusion of being cold, wanting to get this interlude over as quick as possible. Before Vito uttered another word, Robert sensed two things from the sweaty fat man. One, he was under some kind of pressure. Two, his blood was at boiling point. No need for nocturnal mysticism for that analysis though,

Vito's shortness of breath as he began to speak, and obvious anxiety were plastered all over his obese frame.

"Let's take a walk," Vito instructed more than asked. The two headed away from the complex on the path that led to the river. Mortal Robert would have felt nervous about this solitary hike, but immortal Robert was intrigued to see how this was going to play out. Fully confident that he could handle whatever fat boy way going to toss him. Taking quick snapshots to see if anyone was following them, a minute later Vito started to speak, "Hey, I need a quick loan. My son Mikey. Remember him? Always was into cars and shit."

"Yeah, I remember little Mikey. Had that old T-top Camaro, right?" Robert responded.

"Yeah, that fucking thing was a piece of junk. Blew out heads quicker than a junkie whore. Any ways, his wife says I owe them some back rent and since the slut made me sign a lease, she says she can file on me. If it goes to collections, I lose my voucher. Can you believe this shit? My own flesh and blood letting this skifooza pull this stunt?" Vito shouted. They passed the dog park and kept walking onto the long pier that went fifty yards out into the water.

"That's a shame. How much are we talking about here?" Robert responded.

"No biggie, two dimes. You know I'm good for it," Vito explained.

They were now twenty yards onto the sturdy pier, but the wooden planks cried for help under Vito's girth. October winds tailed off of the dark bay, sweeping toward the bright moon that appeared to rise from the sea. Robert knew this day would come. Vito had been hustling for decades, one debacle after another. Robert would pay two thousand and get back a couple hundred here and there. By the time Vito paid back a dime, the debt would be resolved in his thick skull. This was no debt being chased by his daughter in law. Vito's kids were dumber than he was. No way they could put together a proper lease. Deep droplets of sweat streaked from Vito's temple. Oh no, this was a serious debt to some serious people, drug dealers Robert guessed. Robert turned to the fat man and gave his answer,

"Sorry Vito, but I'm going to have to pass."

Robert's unexpected answer hit Vito like a bus that jumped a curb, striking an unsuspecting pedestrian.

"Huh?" Was all Vito could muster in response.

"Yeah man. You know, I could tell you things are tight. I could say I don't have that kind of scratch, but honestly, I just like to see you squirm like this," Robert said.

"Da fuck boy?" Vito replied, if the initial answer smacked him, Robert's explanation was a lethally verbal upper cut. After taking a few steps back to the edge of the pier to size up his target, Vito exploded.

"Da fuck are you talking to like that? Have you lost your fucked up mind? Let's forget about the drinks, dances, and romp I paid for the last week. Oh, you thought she was really into you? Ha! That bitch came back in the morning and jumped me because you were to much of a pussy to get the job done right," Vito proclaimed. Robert had a quick wow moment. Tommy was a true to life rat. Must have told Vito the false play by play that was fed him. The thought passed quickly. Robert tilted his head with a smile, only infuriating the fat man more. Vito started again, "Always thought you was better than all of us didn't you buster? Moved a little more north and made a little more money, but you were nothing but a little bitch when we was little and you're an ungrateful little bitch now."

"Oh really?" Robert questioned. Still adorning a silly smirk, loving every minute of Vito's meltdown. Perspiration was puddling around the top of the fat man's sweatshirt. Sweat stains sprouted from his underarms. Robert could smell his blood start to burn like a freshly lit candle.

"And another thing you might want to know Bobby boy. When you were doing night shift, that pretty little wife of yours was doing half the bar," Vito sprouted with venom.

Several horrific things happened in unnatural haste. Vito's eyes nearly burst quicker than his heart when he saw the man he knew as a kid turn into something that resembled a monster from a creature feature. As the word bar left Vito's mouth, fury exploded from the vampire like lava from a newly erupted volcano. The skin on Robert's face retracted as his mouth protruded. Eager fangs nearly flew out of his mouth. Rage ripped down his arms and spread through newly clawed hands. As fast and furious as his reaction was to Vito's slight, the fat man's death tumble happened faster. If Vito's eyes nearly burst, his heart most certainly did. Robert could actually hear the pop of an artery as Vito fell backwards. Obesity and full-blown stress mixed with seeing a man turn into a beast was a great combination for instant heart eruption. Vito was dead before his backward falling body fell into the bay. Robert made a lunge to catch the fat fuck, but just missed. Dead or not, the furious vampire wanted to chew Vito's face off for insulting his Mary. By the light of the moon, Robert could see his undead reflection in the dark green bay water, as Vito sunk beneath the surface. No dashing count of ancient lore stared back. A fanged-up fiend, with narrow insect shaped black eyes and elongated face reflected from the sea. This was the first time Robert saw himself full on turned. The vision sent him scurrying quickly back to his apartment. A pale human rocket shot off the pier, down the graveled path and looked to collide with the front entrance to The Shores. The short sprint calmed the beast a bit as reason cut into fury. If anyone saw him moving and coming like this, it was all over. At first Robert began to cut left into the woods, then remembered that he left his slider open and cut right, hoped the five-foot brick perimeter in a single bound and darted toward his personal patio.

Three hours and two ice cold showers later, a man finally looked back at Robert in the mirror. If the sweet temptation of blood caused the turn, rage, and anger brough it forth in uncontrollable circumstance. Kyle, Dawn, bank bully, and delivery dick had pissed him off, but dealing with a lifetime of Vito's antics and his filthy final words sent Robert into another state of frenzied emotions. Human hands still held the slightest of trembles as they clutched the bathroom sink. One more glance into the foggy mirror and it was decided, under no circumstance was he leaving the apartment again, until Katie returned.

Chapter Seventeen
October 17th

Sirens and chatter echoed outside of the community, the noise fluttering down the hallways, slipping under the door and clogging Robert's ears. The bums were mired in a classic mid-day pitcher's duel as Robert muted the game and gave a studied listen to the obvious discovery of Vito's late night death dip. The only anxiety to run through the new creature of the night was that of not being able to turn back to some semblance of mortal form after the rage induced transformation from Vito's insults ran rampant through his undead system. No thoughts of consequence raced through the confident vampire's mind. And why should it? He was an obese slob that finally blew a gasket and tumbled into the sea. Loud whispers echoing through the halls brought about new worries. Tommy and Sal had known Vito was with Robert last. They probably knew what Vito was going to be asking for. Was there some motive there? Would the duo point fingers at their old friend? What friend? Robert had not seen either of the men in many years and if not for fat boy's arrival, he would never had said boo to them, though they shared the same building. Eyes closed and head tilted back again, Robert sent a grateful thank you to the heavens. Thankful that big man took a tidal tumble before the monster put claw and fang upon him, leaving some physical evidence that would be difficult to explain. Robert opened his eyes as the slight tremor of anxiety dissipated, he returned sharp pupils to the game. The camera man pointed to dancing fans in the stands. A good-looking mom doing a version of the twist with her young son renewed Robert's focus back to Sasha. He had planned to get some hard evidence tomorrow night, but the night life was getting out of control. Waiting for Katie was the right move. Would she be going out with Matthew away from home? If so, would this not be the perfect time to catch her in the forbidden act? It did not take super sensory ears to hear the thumping of a chopper over the complex. Did they need a chopper to pull his fat ass out of the water? Robert had many drowning victims brought into the E.R. through the years. Repercussions from drunken and clumsy clowns disrespecting the might of the Chesapeake. Remembering that there was always a fly over to scan the area after a corpse or near corpse was pulled from the bay. With the sound back on, he turned up the volume to drown out the resident's chatter and roar from the chopper. Robert picked up his notepad during the current commercial break. Katie was due back any day. What would she make of all that had happened? Should he tell her? Could she simply sense it? He was already pulling deep dark secrets from the scents of the mortals. Being a much older and wiser vampire, Katie could probably instantaneously read his recent past with the ease of digesting a children's pop-up book. What would one more excursion hurt? He would just snap some photos and have a chat with Matthew upon his return from the frigid north. Katie probably had all manner of new rules to follow and adhere by, but Robert knew in his undead heart, that he must make sure his son was informed before disappearing into the night for good. Mind made up and plan formed, he picked up the phone and dialed his son's landline. A chipper Matthew answered via voicemail. Robert left no message. Rolling the dice on fate, he dialed Sasha's cell next.

"Hi Bob," Sasha answered.

"Hey, I was just checking in. I did not hear from Matthew, usually he sends a text or a call letting me know he arrived safely," Robert said. He had not had check in calls from his son since the boy was at University but needed a flicker to light the flame.

"Oh, he's good. Just really busy. You know how those conferences drag on. Usually makes him sleepy, he usually crashes right after he checks into the hotel," Sasha explained.

"Good, good. Hey, do the boys have soccer tomorrow? I was going to come out and watch or give them a lift and take them out for some sweets after, if that is alright?" Robert asked.

"Shoot, wish you would have called earlier. The sitter is taking them and we already paid her for the next two weeks with Matt being gone. I got a lot going on to, with school functions, and tomorrow is my only night to get a break with the girls. But they will be up at Turner field at seven if you want to go watch them. They will be with the sitter till midnight so please don't offer to take them home or out after. She is expensive as hell and needs to earn her money," Sara answered.

"Of course. I will try and get up there. Miss the little guys. Alrighty then, if you need anything while Matthew is gone, don't hesitate to call," Robert said. Sasha thanked him before ending the call abruptly.

This slut has zero respect for her family. The thought of her leaving her children with a stranger to go screw while her husband was out of the country, sent quick red droplet's trickling down the side of Robert's eyes. Sadness, not rage, rose from his stomach, through his dry throat, and muttered sniffles from his nose. There was no explanation or reason for Sasha's betrayal. People fell out of love for sure, but only a selfish vile creature would risk devastation to their own family. A creature with capable reason, that still inflicted pain, was the worst of all. After wiping the thick red tears from his cheek, Robert went to work on a plan. Regardless of his maker's wishes, he would gather the proper proof tomorrow and lay it out for poor Matty when the boy came home.

Vampiric eyes flew from left to right over the yellow legal pad for the fifth time. He was pleased with the plan. Fairly simply in and out job. Get the photos he needed and get out. A quick stop at the pet store earlier in the day as well, thinking a furry nibble would hold back any blood drunk desires, should the site of his foul daughter in law and her lard ass lover ignite a terror transformation. BANG, BANG, BANG. Holy shit, Vito had returned from his tidal tomb, was Robert's first thought. Quickly dismissed as the voices behind the door announced the arrival of law enforcement. A juggernaut of scenarios speed through Robert's mind. After a few seconds of heavy breathing, the vampire relaxed, knowing that there was nothing to hide. He opened the door with aggression and asked the two plain clothed officers in. Detective Ronson was a short stout fellow that wore his self-important stature with more pride than his cheap blue sport coat. Detective Starkes was much better suited to the job and better dressed as well. Starkes was at least six-foot-five, black as the night itself, with impeccable ivory teeth to match his impeccably ironed grey suit. Ronson had to be pushing sixty and most likely the joker was only in a detective position through years of just outlasting anyone around him. Starkes may just have been forty. His demeanor alluded to a much higher ranking or political position in the very near future. Robert gaged all of this in under a minute, from the duo's physical and metaphysical approaches into his apartment. The hesitant host offered them a drink. Both declined and took an offered seat in the living room on the far side of the sofa, across from Robert's favorite spot. The inquisition began.

"Mr. Robinson, did you see Vito Vitalli last night?" Ronson questioned. The stooge damn well knew Robert had been with him. The stench of boredom flew off of his cheap clothes. Ronson obviously just wanted to run the gauntlet of questions and go home.

"Yes, we had a late-night walk," Robert answered.

"About what time did you last see him?" Ronson asked, this time with a long yawn in between words. Robert was happy to see the disinterest from Ronson, but was wary of Starkes silence.

"Damn. Around eight or nine. I'm retired. Time has a way of losing yourself when you have no place to be," Robert answered again.

"What state was mister Vitalli in, when you last spoke?" Ronson prodded.

"Maryland," Robert responded. A mistake, the joke caused both men of the law to stop the routine round of questions. Both lawman shot disapproving glares toward their host.

"Sorry, Sorry. I know what you mean. He seemed fine. Not at all under the influence or anything like that," Robert explained. Taking on a more serious demeanor.

"We are assuming you know he drowned last night?" Starkes asked, finally interjecting.

"Yeah, Yeah. I heard from some residents. When a pet dies it's like a major news story around here. Vito drowning might just be the story of the decade to us bored old people," Robert replied.

"You don't appear to be that upset. Was he not a good friend of yours?" Starkes continued. Taking over the show with a strong voice to accompany his large imposing frame.

"Good Friend? Nah, I hadn't seen him for many years until he moved in here a couple weeks ago. We were just chatting about sports. He liked sitting on the pier at night. It was chilly, so I headed back early. Last I saw him, he looked fine, walking up and down the pier," Robert answered.

"Your other buddies say he was into some narcotics. By any chance did he mention taking anything that night or offer you any drugs?" Ronson asked, stepping back into the fold of questioning. Not needing any supernatural senses to know that Ronson wanted this over and done with quickly, while the intelligent Starkes was sensing something afoot. Starkes unflinching stare started to make Robert uncomfortable. Robert quickly decided to give blunt answers to hurry the law men out of his home.

"Vito was into everything. Drink. Women. Drugs. But to be honest, last night he was sober as a judge. He knew I never did anything but drink, so he had never offered me any drugs at any time," Robert sprouted quickly.

Ronson looked at his tablet and started another mundane question when Starkes cut him off with a large, raised hand.

"That will be all Mr. Robinson. Thank you for taking the time to answer our inquires. It appears Mr. Vitalli simply had a heart attack or stroke and was dead before he hit the water," Starkes stated. The two officers rose in unison with Ronson and headed for the door.

"At his weight and age, it was bound to happen sooner or later. I worked in the medical field my entire career, seen it thousands of times. You have got to take care of yourself," Robert stated.

"Well, you certainly take care of yourself Mr. Robinson. Our records have you at seventy years of age. You do not look a day over fifty," Starkes said.

"Thank you, Mr. Starkes, good diet and exercise is all it takes. And keeping busy, keeping your mind and body busy is key," Robert responded. He opened the door and the detectives walked slowly into the hallway before turning back toward him.

"You have certainly kept busy Mr. Robinson." Starkes said, with a sly smile.

"How do you mean?" Robert questioned.

"Well, a call came into the local department a few days ago. Some store manager ranting about you threatening her staff. One witness stated that your face actually changed, and you hissed at her through a set of deadly fangs," Starkes stated, turning to his partner as they shared a little giggle. Robert tilted his head down to mask his initial response, he faked a laugh as well. His head rose and he explained.

"Yeah, well, for the first time in my life, I really lost my temper. Been on a rough road since my wife passed a while back. I Promise, you will not get any more calls regarding me," Robert explained. He painted a stoic face on his flesh mask to resonate the point. The detectives took a slight step backwards before Starkes finished the interview.

"Yeah, yeah, we heard about your wife. Very sorry for your loss Mr. Robinson. We may be by again for our follow up report. See, when somebody is the last person around a dead man, we must put a full inquiry into the system. I am sure you understand. Do you have any plans to leave the area in the immediate future?" Starkes said.

"Not at all. Sure, sure, I get it. Come by anytime and thank you for your condolences," Robert said. The three nodded in unison before Robert closed the door gently in disgust.

Chapter Eighteen
October 18th

That Starkes was one sharp tack. Robert kept mulling over the encounter until beams of early dawn crept into the apartment. After the two detectives left, an hours long game of what to do now began and Robert was the only contestant. Questions and scenarios sprung up and around him like fresh Petunias begging for the early heat of spring. How did they know that his wife had passed? If they knew that, how much of a background check did they do on him? Why did no officers visit him after he was reported from Dollar Land? What did Tommy and Sal tell the cops? Should he still proceed with tonight's Sasha stalking session? Where the fuck was Katie? It was seven AM until Robert finally laid to rest, equal parts satisfied with his rational answers and his concocted plan to put an end to his son's miserable marriage. Once more he replayed reason before settling in for the day. They knew his wife passed because they had to run a standard background check on any person who was last seen with a floating corpse. No one came after the Dollar Land debacle because no one was going to listen to those idiots. Especially after it checked out that a Seventy-year-old, former medical professional, with no prior criminal record, who apparently morphed into a monster, was of any threat. The police had to tell them to just call back if Robert ever came around again. Tommy and Sal did not say shit. Both would not want anything to do with getting in trouble with the law, nor risk their housing vouchers being taken away. All they probably said was that Vito was walking with him the last they heard. Yes, he had to get his proof tonight. He knew where she would be. What time she would be there, and he only needed a quick shot or two and then he could start his new life in peace, all scores settled. Katie? Yeah Katie? Who the hell knows? He would give it one more week until he would let panic pour in like water bursting through a broken dam. Robert, mind at peace, rolled over for his sunshine slumber, his eyes fell upon his wedding day photo and for the first time no emotion rang a response. That life was truly over. After closing his eyes, the rest of his new nocturnal body slipped instantly into a comatose state, except for the slight swelling in his throat.

Parched lips parted as Robert let out a long deep yawn. Pitch black darkness blanketed the bedroom, pouring over the undead body that inhabited it. The vampire felt refreshed after the long rest. The time announced from the phone sent shivers of panic through Robert's pale frame. Seven PM. He was beyond running late. The boys started their practice at seven. He should have been waiting in the woods by now. Forgoing a refreshing ice-cold shower, Robert flew at unnatural speed to prepare for his exit. Phone was fully charged, thank the stars. If his cell went out before he could snap some photos, the entire plan was deader than Vito. He threw on his best stalking attire. Matching all black sweat pants and top, with black sneakers, and a black wool cap. A quick glance in the mirror showed the vampire looking like some low budget supernatural criminal about to go on a caper. Phone and plan in hand, Robert swiftly made way out of the apartment, down the hall and out of The Shores lobby at a speed that looked odd to the few residents that caught a blurred vision of their unnatural neighbor.

Twenty minutes later, Robert parked his car at the last space in the back of the nearly deserted parking lot of the convenience store. Confident he was still on schedule, it was not even eight yet, he took a minute to compose himself. A quick peep in the mirror reflected a pale taunt face looking back. The thirsty vampire started to look emaciated again, his mouth was dryer than sandpaper. It had only been three days since he took a bite of Blankenship. Katie had said a mouthful would do for a week. Perhaps his mortal age dissipated the blood quicker. Several red stained pisses the last couple days gave merit to that theory. A wicked blast of fall air refreshed the creature of the night as he walked to the convenient store first. Robert wanted to dine on a mouse before his stalking session, but the exhaustion from playing the cops inquiry over and over caused him to sleep well past his desired start time. Two middle aged women dressed for the night shot him a wanting look as Robert made way to the cooler. After grabbing a Gatorade, he walked quickly past the two ladies toward the register.

"Hey buddy, what you up to tonight?" One of the women questioned.

"Trouble," Robert responded.

The women let out a hoot first, followed by silence. Robert's eyes had met theirs. His black beaded unnatural pupils had quickly dampened their desires. A bored teenager checked him out at the register before Robert guzzled the entire red colored juice as he left the front of the store. The sports drink did give his thirst an ounce of relief and the cool drink mixed with the cool air settled his nerve. Last time Robert hugged the side of the road until he approached the Wolves Den motel. This time he took a direct and more hidden route through the thick woods. Scurrying sounds erupted through the thick brush as soon as the supernatural being stepped on the first fallen branch. The apex predator had entered their domain, in response, the creatures of the forest knew to get out of town quick. A few minutes later, Robert was back between the two huge bushes that covered him from the glowing lights of the shitty motel. This Monday was very different than his first trip to the sleaze palace. Only an insanely tall, rail thin, young woman adorned the front of the place. She strode back and forth between the chipped painted doors with eager anticipation for her date. After the initial shock at the mere sight of the giant lady, frustration flowed through the vampire's undead skin. Not a car in his immediate sight and no sign of her pearl white Benz. Just the flicker from a cheap T.V. set from the manager's office, glowed in the parking lot. The sight of the Beamer brought brief relief, doctor dickhead was here. But where the fuck was Sasha? Robert waited with baited patience for twenty minutes. The giant's ride picked her up, his old shoeless buddy, the manager, took a smoke break in the empty parking lot, yet still no sign of his disgusting daughter in law. After floating around a few scenarios, Robert decided to hug the outline of the forest and go around the back to test his supernatural hearing senses. If the front of The Den was shoddy, the back of the place was a complete disaster. It looked like a bomb of pill bottles, needles, and beer cans was set off. The back of the rooms had sliding doors, covered with cheap curtains that lead out about thirty yards to another side of the forest. Robert gingerly avoided the cavalcade of litter, snuck past the back of the manager's office, then grabbed the stucco wall that sat outside the good doctor's temporary home. It was her! Overly exuberant moaning blasted beyond the cheap glass door, exploding into Robert's eardrums. He could hear the steady thumping of the mattress as Sasha rode the fat man. Moments later the bouncing and moaning ceased, followed by childlike giggles. Robert started a retreat to his pre-determined camp out sight, prepared to get the shots he needed to set his son free. He began a contemplation as to where her car was when an old voice interrupted him.

"You again! You sick mother fuckkkkkkk…" The manager tried to yell.

Before the manager could complete his foul-mouthed sentence, Robert was on him, throwing a quick left jab, which was his signature move when a struck batter would charge him on occasion. Blood poured from a destroyed nose and the shoeless man flew backward five yards. The fully formed vampire pounced on him at once, merely wanted to silence the prick, but the fountain of blood turned reason into madness and the night beast started licking the delicious flowing puddle from chin to nostril. The manager came to and attempted to squirm out of the freak's grasp. A roar exploded into the night as Robert felt a sharp object slice into the side of his stomach. Manager had managed to get a hold of a broken beer bottle and stabbed the beast in the belly. In response, Robert swopped his left claw across the face of the blood-soaked man, snapping his neck instantly. More blood began to seep from the swipe, three sharp fingernails had opened up the man's cheek on impact. Robert put his mouth on the man's tilted dead head, letting the new wound pour through his snarled lips. This blood was tainted with strong cheap liquor and every drug known to man, the effects rippled through the vampire, causing an instant, immortal, euphoric high.

"What the fuck!" The good doctor shouted. The noise caused him to peak outside. He discovered two men locked in a blood kiss.

Dressed only in his silk boxer shorts, the doctor attempted to turn toward the safety of his room when a pale flesh flash bolted right at his mid-section. With some reason left, Robert turned toward the doctor and went for the semi-hard cock that rested below his enormous belly. With one leap and another right swipe, Robert removed the man's manhood. The doctor went into shock as his remaining genitalia sprouted a red waterfall. Before he could let out another yelp, Robert rose and jammed all ten of his taloned fingers into the fat fuck's neck. Phlegm and blood speckled the vampire's face as he came face to face with the man who had disrespected his family. One more slight jerking motion and the vampire nearly took the obese doctor's head clean off. Blood drunk crazed, he tossed his prey to the side and stealthy entered the cheap room. Strong scents of sex and industrial air freshener bounced off the walls. The hissing sound of the shower gave away Sasha's location. The night beast made his way to her, his stomach wound already scabbing over.

"Babe. What was that loud ass sound? Is there black bears up here?" Sasha shouted over the streaming water.

Robert crept through the foggy room and tore the plastic curtain from right to left. Nude, head back, rinsing her hair, and neck exposed, Sasha allowed the warm water to cascade down her thin frame. Before striking, the vampire wanted her to see him, see his new face, see what her betrayal had done. Robert stole a quick glance at her body, once again in disbelief that she could satisfy her husband with those small tits that hung just above her ribs. No wonder she wanted a boob job was one of the last mortal thoughts he had before his attack. Sasha tilted her head down and opened her soap-stained eyes. Her body quivered in fear. Hot piss ran down one slender tanned leg. Robert stepped slowly into the tub. Before she could let out a scream, he dug into her temple with both hands as he jerked her head back. A quick head jerk forward and both fangs punctured Sasha's neck. Blood instantly flew with force from her mouth, spackling the ceiling. Robert sucked with the strength of a hundred lords. Sasha's blood burst into his lower mouth, only a small stream missed, which slowly poured down her nude dying body. Robert felt the moment all life was gone, he withdrew, and let out another ravaging roar. Wood paneled walls three doors down rattled to the tune of the beast bellow. The heat from the shower ran out. Ice-cold water fell over woman and vampire. Sasha's limp arms hung over his shoulders. Her head slumped into his heaving chest. Seconds felt like minutes, minutes felt like hours, but after a while Robert snapped back into some semblance of reason as he placed his dead daughter in law flat in the tub. The freezing stream of water started cleansing her of what little blood was left on her body. Dazed and soaked, Robert walked over to the shabby queen-sized bed and sat. Moments later he removed his wet blood-stained head from his blood-stained hands and started to clean up.

Pure ecstasy, fear, and the remnants of whatever the manager snorted earlier raced through the vampire as he executed his quick plan. If he got caught, he got caught, giving no illusion to the consequences. Robert squirmed as the wound from his quickly healing side stung like a bad wasp sting, throbbing as he picked up the manager. The wounded creature darted to the entrance of the blackened forest. A few minutes later the quick-thinking vampire picked up Sasha and sprinted back into the wooded abyss. Another few minutes later and he shoved the severed cock into the doctor's arm pit, picked up the obese man, and made way once more to his exit strategy. Even with supernatural strength, the weight of the doctor caused Robert to labor during his final excursion. With the three bodies lying next to the river bank, the night beast took a moment to gaze up at the full moon. He recalled the couple dozen times, from his mortal life, sitting in on reports from murder victims that clung to life when they entered the E.R. and perished. His first plan was to bury all three deep, but the blood trail and the eventual discovery by cadaver dogs or ground radar would send law enforcement on a mad man hunt. Still blood high, Robert tried to generate a best-case scenario. A quick trip back to the sight of his first attack of the night, Robert grabbed the broken beer bottle before sprinting back the three miles from which he came as if the devil himself were chasing him. Using the bottle, Robert applied few slashes to Sasha's neck and the doctor's lower regions. Once satisfied, the vampire tossed them both into the north flowing current of the river, like a garbage man would a light load of trash. After smashing the manager's head a few times into some of the jagged rocks that sat on the bank of the water, Robert rested him head first into the cool reservoir, keeping his body land locked. With supernatural night vision, he caught one last glance of Sasha's bobbing brunette hair as the current took her around a bend and out of sight forever. Oddly, he felt great about seeing her washed away, in fact, he felt a demon's delight.

Chapter Nineteen
October 19th

A blood-soaked foul fiend reflected from the rearview mirror. Robert hardly recognized himself. The massive intake of blood combined with jubilant ecstasy caused his forehead and cheekbones to protrude, his mouth to resend, eye lids to narrow. A snake like reptile replaced the mug of a human being. Grasping the steering wheel, a concentrated attempt was made to regain mortal focus. After exiting the banks of the blood bath, Robert flew through the dark dim woods, only the curse filled clamoring of several bikers looking for the manager interrupted his flee as the night beast galloped past the Den toward his car. Sitting at a red light with eyes closed, serenity fell over the monster as he reexamined the sinister situation. The call from the babysitter would probably come an hour after midnight, it was a little after nine now. Christ, he thought, the entire evil events took place in under an hour. It would be at least until dawn before even the pinnacle of the police would come looking for him. Plenty of time to gather a few things, get some quick cash out and attempt an escape. Desperately hoping Katie would be able to track him. She had mentioned something about being around Binghamton, New York. Robert would start his search there. At pace and with the luck of the devil on his side, he estimated getting there by four in the morning. Before the light of day and tonight's terror would eventually drain him to exhaustion. Stage two of the blood high kicked in along with more reason. Fingernails, facial bones, and fangs retracted to their human factory settings. Just the fantastic, frenzied flow of his victim's blood coursing through a fully filled undead body gave a tangible reminder that Robert was still a creature of darkness and not a mortal man. Back on the road, thoughts turned to his baby boy as he rocked back and forth at each red light. The bliss of the blood took hold. Captured, killed, or off to a new life in the shadows, one way or another he would get an explanation to Matthew.

The Shores parking lot sat silent except for the night birds that chirped around the wooded path at the back of the complex. With heightened hearing, Robert listened to the swooping of owls as they dove from their branched perches to feed on the insect below them. An odd analogy to the apex predator that he had become. A quick examination revealed that dried blood was blanketed all over his black sweatsuit attire, not much on his person though as he gulped most of it with glee. A slight tear in the heavy shirt, where the manager poked him, gave little cause for concern. Robert removed the sweatshirt, thankful for wearing his black t-shirt underneath, but regretted not leaving his patio door unlocked before rushing out into the naughty night. With new strength, it would be easy to rip the door open, but the complex was triggered with alarms upon any forced entry. Clicking off the interior overhead lights in the car, the creeping creature pulled his woolly hat down low. Robert felt confident he could stroll quickly to his apartment without garnering much attention. The lobby was bright and empty, a welcomed relief. Turning the corner, a new but familiar voice greeted him from the entrance to the media room.

"A tad chilly for an undershirt? is it not? Mr. Robinson?" Starkes questioned. Robert turned, warm blood that pumped through him went instantly to ice. With a welcoming smile and quick wit, Robert responded.

"My grandkid threw up on my sweatshirt. How are you Mr. Starkes?"

"Great, really great. Could I speak with you for a few minutes? Nothing major, just want to finish our report on Mr. Vitalli," Starkes replied.

"Sure, you are always welcomed in my home," Robert said.

"We can just sit in here. Like I said. Only a few final questions. Won't take but a few minutes," Starkes responded.

Robert acceptingly nodded as he walked past the imposing detective, catching the aroma of an expensive cologne that sprung off of the sophisticated man's collar. Three of the old guard's club seized their spirited game of Pinnacle, turning their inquisitive eyes toward the odd duo. Old lady glances silently jeered and judged under swollen wrinkled lids. Robert planted in the first cushioned chair closet to the exit, careful to turn slightly to the right as not to show the small rip and dried specks of blood that sprinkled the side of his stomach. Starkes took post in another to the left. No tablet or tiny notepad to aid in his inquisition, Starkes had his oral examination glued inside his intelligent head.

He began softly. "Do you know a Laura DeMarco?"

Robert tilted his head to the side and responded, "No, I do not know anyone named Laura."

Starkes stifled a small laugh before starting again, "Sorry, she goes by the name of Luna to many. Does that name sound familiar?"

Robert took a longer than expected pause in attempt to catch any mystical intent coming from the detective. Sasha stunk of deceit, Vito of gluttony, and the Middle Eastern man, who gave Robert his first taste of sensory projection, reeked of fear. Starkes masked his emotion with highly trained collectiveness and calming demeanor. Sensing his routine answer giving away the goods, Robert snapped back to business at hand. "Yes, I know Luna well."

"Ms. DeMarco speaks very highly of you. She did say that you did not like Vito very much, is that true?" Starkes asked.

"Look. Like. Not like. The guy was an old friend from the neighborhood. Our lives took very different paths. I actually felt sorry for the guy," Robert responded.

Starkes laughed again. "Different paths? By all accounts you were one of the top nurses in the region, a great father, husband, and one hell of a ballplayer. Vito was a no-good degenerate pimp who sold narcotics to children. Perhaps he deserved to get murdered. To be honest Mr. Robinson, myself nor anyone on the force could give a shit about that fat asshole. I'm just curious as to your role in any of this."

"Did you say murdered?" Robert questioned. Already slightly trembling from the blood high, when Starkes said the word murdered, Robert recognized stage one of the turn beginning, triggered by rising anxiety. Starkes explained,

"Well. the way I see it, maybe Vito wasn't murdered. I mean the man was a ticking medical time bomb. But some real weird stuff keeps popping up around you. Six years in military intelligence makes one eager for answers. Makes one look past the obvious. To be honest Mr. Robinson, I questioned my own sanity until I spoke with Ms. DeMarco. We ran a quick check on you after finding out you were the last to see Vito. Just so happened a sergeant I know responded to the call about you at Dollar Land. He said there was an odd honesty about the tall tale that the lady told about you. You know, about turning into some kind of monster. I brushed it off before meeting you. I mean, the digital check on you was impressive, not even a vehicle violation. Mr. Robinson you were a social studies video for how a human being should live. Then I saw you. These days, thirty is the new twenty, forty is the new thirty, but could seventy be the new fifty? I mean for the love of me, I cannot see one damn wrinkle, only a hint of grey, and not an ounce of fat on you. Still, after I left your apartment, I figured a man of medicine knows biological secrets, a former athlete would keep in good shape, and I've seen plenty of Asians during my tours that made ninety look like fifty. All that clean raw food and mediation. But, after I spoke with Luna yesterday, I had to really dig and make some weird calls to some high-ranking people. I got even weirder answers. Luna really digs you, said you are a complete gentleman. She is hoping you will give her a call. After being up for over forty hours mulling this situation over, I had to keep prying just a bit more before letting it go. Seen a ton of girls looking for a good man to take care of them and their kids, but something was still off. It did not take my master's in psychology to get her to open up more. To be fair, she admitted to being drunk as a skunk, but when I asked if anything out of the ordinary had happened, she said things may have gotten a bit rough. When she showered after returning from your place, Luna swore there were tiny, crusted pieces of what looked like blood, that fell from her hair. Now here's the kicker. She thinks you may have bitten her tit, even showed me two tiny, discolored spots, that were healing nicely. Have to say, that quick peep was worth the trip over to her apartment. Robert, I just want to do one harmless exercise. If nothing happens, I promise to walk out of here and never bother you again. May I?"

Starkes was more than well trained. Robert spent many years consulting at the puzzle box, learning all manner of speech hypnosis. The detective nearly put him in a trance like state with his methodic tone. If not for his full meal earlier, Robert would have been near mentally comatose. As such, he was alert, frightened, eager to defend himself.

"Sure, yeah, what do you have in mind?" Robert asked. His undead skin sizzling with anticipation.

Starkes smiled as he reached inside his sport coat. Strong, thick black fingers pulled out a silver letter opener.

"I only want to place this in your bare hand for five seconds."

Robert smiled before sticking out his trembling left hand. Starkes leaned in to place the pointed small dagger in it when Robert struck. A full force right cross that instantly dislocated the detective's jaw. Starkes, with remarkable resolve, recovered quickly. The detective shot out a right footed kick into the creature's chest. The blow knocked the vampire back three yards. Starkes steadied his look, jaw hanging disproportionately to the right of his upper lips, like a Picasso print. All manner of the highest caliber of physical and mental training, all the warnings he received, yet barely believed earlier in the day, did nothing to protect the detective from the beast attack. Turned instantly by his new internal fight response, Robert lounged at Starkes, biting full down from the top of the large man's nose through to the top of his intact upper lip. Loud gurgling replaced a scream, as Robert chewed the man's face off rapidly. The blood of a proper warrior seeping into the mouth of the monster. Screams did interrupt the sensational snack. A quick glance showed the three old bags scrambling toward the back window. No other exit available except past the mythical creature. A quick swipe across the law man's neck ended the interview. Window open and screen popped out, one of the ladies was already half way out of the window. In unnatural speed, Robert met his fellow resident. He greeted her by slamming the window with force down onto her back. The crack of her spine rang louder than the split wood. The glass splintered in two upon the strike. Cowering like cowardly cows, the other two ladies slid and sat pinned against the back wall. A hint of mortality crept into the vampire's soul, but visions of these types from his past made up the monster's mind. Pathetic flesh puppets. Same sad existence, just different printed animal pants. Know it all bitches that lived on the misery of others. Smashing their heads together with fierce force, their skulls instantly shattered, a quick death was better than they deserved Robert concluded. With supernatural speed the vampire made for his home, ready to gather a few things and leave the carnage and mortal world behind for good.

Burps stumbled consistently out of the blood drunk vampire's mouth, each gag rising from Robert's throat spewing speckles of blood on his carpet. He over drank for sure, his chest and bottom stomach swelled with the night's feast swarming through his system. The blood of the detective was exquisite, rich with strength and knowledge. What Mary would have called a brilliant bold red. Two photos of his love sat atop two debit cards along with one credit card. Ever the pragmatist, each card had a four hundred dollar withdraw limit, enough to get him north, hopefully affording Robert the luxury of an out of the way motel room while he could start his search for Katie. With the gym bag filled, plan in place, Robert headed to the bathroom for a quick wash up. Waiting for the lukewarm water to cool, a long look in the mirror was shocking calming. Fifty? Robert looked not a day over thirty, chalked up to the rejuvenating power from his red rampage. Not just a mystical physical transformation took place but an emotional one as well. There was no more anxiety. No more self-pity. No more fear. No more cowardice. No more remorse in the deserved suffering of those that challenged him. Sasha paid for their betrayal. The motel manager and Vito paid for their weak gluttonous lifestyle. The three ladies paid for a lifetime of finger pointing, back stabbing, arrogant behavior. Starkes? What of the brave, wise warrior? Did he deserve such a fate? For suspecting what he would be up against, yet still having the arrogance to confront that. Yes, he fucking did! Lowering his smiling face toward the sink, Robert caught the now cold water in attached clawed palms and splashed the water on his young face several times. A last longing look in the mirror showed the birth of a confident, strong, deadly, monster of myth.

A powerful scent of gasoline crept into the apartment, but the vampire quickly dismissed it. Robert sat his large gym bag down and thumbed through the few personal effects he just had to have. Three financial cards, two photos of Mary, his wedding and school rings, and a gold cross his mother had given him at first holy communion. Holding the sacred symbol in hand triggered a quick reflection. Never filled with faith, Robert had to ponder, if Vampires were real, was God real as well? If so, what kind of God would create such beings? Full of violence, lust, and ego. What kind of God would create human beings? Heat. Strong heat was coming from the hallway. Heat along with the gagging odor of pure gasoline. With zero concern about a possible fire, Robert stuffed his personal keepsakes into the gym bag and started for the sliding door, desperately needing the cover of darkness to avoid any more confrontations. The sound of heavy footsteps jogging toward his door stopped him in his tracks. Supernatural senses on full alert, the vampire knew someone was heading with purpose to his home. Robert dropped the gym bag, shocked himself with the new found ease to turn. With taloned hands out, fangs out, the monster was about to greet unwanted company with a death kiss. Company greeted him with one. It all happened in blinding speed but appeared in slow motion. The door being shouldered inward, flying into the wall to the left. A giant dark man with serpents for hair landing an uppercut to Robert's chin. Blinking snapshots of being carried in the darkness of the back of the community fluttered through his undead eyes. An apartment community that was now engulfed in flames.

Chapter Twenty
October 20th

It was in poor taste, but Ronson lite up his cigarette in desperate attempt to alleviate the images that stained his eyelids. Nine dead, two more that would probably not last the week. This was the total casualty report from the fire. Curious as to why he was sent over at first, the news that Starkes was among the deceased got the stout man moving quicker than he had in decades. Heads torn in two by bullets, limbs severed in car accidents, countless bloated overdose victims, the veteran detective had seen his fair share of horrors over the last thirty years. Twenty hours after seeing the first crispy corpse, Ronson exhaled with a spot of dried vomit flying over his lower lip. A few chunky pieces of regurgitated cereal landed on his chin. Trying to shake the mental shots out of his head was useless. Charred flesh plastered on old bodies and the odor of burnt hair would not leave his mind, nor nostrils. It was the sight of Starkes which frightened his very soul to its core. His partner's skin was scorched to the bone, ivory sticks protruded through caked scabbed flesh. Another coughing fit ensued as Ronson recalled the sight of his friend's face. Starkes's skull appeared indented from the flames, but what made no logical sense was the separation of the lower jaw from the top portion of what remained of the large man's head. An experienced medical examiner's first response was that Starkes must have hit a table or the floor with full force in attempt to flee the fire. Another long puff on a menthol stirred up another acidic rise from his stomach.

Ronson was ready to full on hurl his insides out when the lead fire investigator spoke.

"Commercial grade acetylene detective."

"English please son," Ronson instructed.

"Simply. A gasoline that burns at the highest temperature the quickest. Usually used for shaping steel. Cut through the drywall and laminate floors like a knife through warm butter. That's why the sprinkler system had little effect. Flames were dancing at about fifty-one-hundred degrees," The investigator explained.

"Jesus Christ," Ronson spat. He turned toward two older men, one thin, one massively overweight, being wrangled in by one of his sergeants. Ronson gave the fire investigator a nod and sent him back to the scene. The two men, looking dazed and anxious, greeted the lawman.

"Detective, glad you are here. How the fuck could this happen?" Sal asked.

"Still figuring that out. Thank you for coming to see me. I know this has been a very difficult day," Ronson responded.

"Shit, my tire having a flat is a difficult day, this is a super shitstorm. I'm on the other side of the building, but Tommy here lost everything," Sal said.

Tommy nodded silently, then spoke, "They got spots open at a few of their other communities. I'm going over there tonight with my daughter to look."

"Good, good. Hey, look gentlemen, I know you got a lot to take care of, but I got just a few questions," Ronson asked. Wanting to get to the point quickly before the odd duo continued an empathetic tangent. Sal and Tommy nodded as Ronson began his questioning.

"Did you see Robert Robinson at all last night?" Both men looked at each other, then in unison, shook their heads side to side, signaling a no.

Sal spoke up, "Nah, Bob kind of disappeared after Vito died."

"Did either of you see detective Starkes, the large man that was with me last time I spoke with both of you, last night, or the day before?" Two tired old faces shook their heads no again. Ronson continued. "Have either of you noticed any strange or unusual behavior from Mr. Robinson?"

Sal replied," Ya know what. Ever since he changed up his look, he has been kind of different."

"Changed up his look?" Ronson asked.

"Yeah, he dyed his hair. He was obviously using some kind of expensive skin treatment to make his face look younger. I was thinking he was trying to date again, you know, fill the void after his wife died. I saw him around when he first moved in here, but I paid him no mind. Bob looked like a morose corpse walking through the halls. When Vito got in here, he says we should reach out to the guy.

Next thing I know, Bob looks totally different, he's drinking, fooling with girls. Not the guy I knew. I mean, I liked the new Bob better, the old Bob was a bit of an arrogant asshole. Was Bob and your partner in the fire?" Sal said.

"We are still identifying the bodies and doing an intricate investigation. We should have some news in the next day or so," Ronson answered.

Sal looked back toward the parking lot, let out a sigh, and spoke again with angst. "Shit. Bob's car is still here. He's dead, isn't he?"

"We will have it wrapped up in the next day or two Mr. Pantino. Thank you both for your time. I will pray for you to get back on your feet soon Mr. Durant," Ronson answered.

The two old friends shook the detective's hand and spoke loudly as they walked away with more questions than some of the answers they wanted. Ronson pulled out his phone and dialed the number that he had tried at least six times before, the same voicemail stated that Matthew Robinson was not available and to please leave a detailed message for an appropriate response. Strong gusty winds came hurtling off the water in the distant, the force of the gust shot through Ronson, nearly knocking him over. The cool blast from mother nature helped dissipate the crude images that were still fluttering through his thoughts. A nice walk and sit down was exactly what the detective needed. He saw the benches near the pier and made haste toward one of them, each step toward the scenic view physically assisting in his regained focus. Thoughts turned toward the last two days with Starkes. Gazing out over the rough bay, Ronson pulled another cancer stick from his coat and reflected on his friend's odd behavior. Starkes was a serious man, a serious man with a serious plan. The two had been together just over a year. Ronson knew his partner was just filling in the dots with his current position before taking a high-end federal job. Both of them would be gone from the department by January. Ronson to live the good life down in Sarasota. Starkes off to a position that was more suited to his intelligence and experience. His now deceased partner was a quiet man, but Starkes's silence after the meeting with Robinson was eerie. Thirteen months with the man and Ronson knew not to ask any questions. The fat guy blew a gasket, the old man Robinson was nervous because he probably witnessed it and walked away from someone he could care less about. That had to be the reason for his antsy behavior. Starkes sensed something else and Ronson let him be. Over the summer the superior intelligent, militarily trained, detective, had unraveled a murder mystery involving an unsuspecting cousin of a victim. After that display, along with the half-dozen other cases Starkes unraveled at ease, Ronson just sat back and quietly admired the man. The two would often work separately as Starkes enjoyed the hunt, attacking each case with indominable intellect. Always, always, there was a text, call, or email from Starkes, checking in. The last two days, nothing. Ronson chalked it up to perhaps his partner being called into Langley for some consultation, but even during those brief trips, Starkes still checked in with him. Ronson's admiration and respect for the man probably got him killed, or perhaps he too would have suffered the same flamed fate. Tossing his smoke into the weeds, the tired man stood and was about to head back for more answers when the robotic ping from his phone signaled the commander's call.

"Hey Billy, what's the news?" The commander questioned.

"Nothing much. Count is final at nine down, including Starkes. The other two have hours to live," Ronson answered.

"And the guy Robinson?" The commander asked.

"Well, there were four males total. Our boy and two of the others have family that have not heard from them. Leaving only one male not identified. Inspector has to get dental in here for identification. I got a bullshit resident list from one of the maintenance guys. The office staff are being shut down from their corporate office due to the weak ass sprinkler system that failed miserably. They are only giving one-word answers for now. I've called Robinson's son several times, still voicemail. He had no one else in his database for me to try and reach out to," Ronson answered.

"Billy, I know you've been out there awhile, but we need to find out if this man is still at large."

"At large? You really think this guy set the blaze?"

"We got a call from county. Two bodies pulled from Darkbluff river, one more on the banks of the water with their face bashed in. More good news, one of the bodies is Robinson's daughter in law."

"Jesus Christ on a bicycle. You think Starkes was following him and saw that go down?"

"I don't know what the hell to think. All I got is that Starkes was probably doing a follow up to close the Vitalli case, got caught in a freak fire, and died. That is all we give anyone right now. Fuck the coroner's report, I think this old man flipped his shit. Killed this guy Vito, went after his daughter in law, then torched the place when he saw Starkes. Didn't you tell me the guy looked way younger and insanely fitter than a man of his age?"

"Yeah, it was kind of freaky, but we knew he worked in medicine. Most of those types keep a healthy lifestyle. Didn't think too much of it at the time. The guy just didn't seem the type to be involved in anything like this," Ronson explained.

The commander continued. "Well, the fire chief told me someone just dumped this high-grade shit from lobby entrance through to one of the exits and lite a match. I've seen some sick shit, but there has got to be some god damn motive for someone to lite up a senior apartment community. Look, I need you to keep it together down there through the night. Feds around in a few hours to assist. Whoever did this knew the building as well, surveillance looks to be wiped."

"What? The security cams didn't have back up to the alarm companies?" Ronson asked.

"Looks like they ran cheap across the board. Most of these communities are tax credit. Not bound to code. Just hang tight, see what you can sniff out. Main priority is to get me the info on if that last body is Robinson asap." The commander explained.

"Will do boss. I got Sullivan and Tomkins asking around the facility now. Some of the residents on the other side of the complex are filtering back in. Any details come in, I will check in immediately," Ronson replied.

"Thanks Billy, you and the boys be careful walking around in there. That place has to have been built by the lowest bidder with the cheapest material. I know you really took to Starkes. He was a great man. We will sort this out," The commander commanded, then hung up, the way important men do.

Ronson walked back toward the wooded area away from the complex to have another smoke. After twenty-six years of honest good work, Ronson was the first to admit that he was punching a clock the last four. Equal parts exhaustion and frustration at pushing against the inevitable demise of human decay. Three months until long nights and sleepy days on the surf. Now a moral dilemma was sent from above, or possibly from below. So close to retirement, the boss would let him take a backseat until he turned in his badge. Nothing he could do could bring back Starkes, but the oddity of the case and death of an honorable man hit too hard for him to take a seat on the bench. One more investigation, one more trip down the rabbit hole. This was the pitiful plot of every bad cop television show or film ever made.

Chapter Twenty-One
October 21st

Matty and Marco chased the round black and white ball around the backyard with reckless abandon. Both clattering into each other while their grandfather sipped his beer and laughed. Robert never could grasp the fanatical obsession with soccer. At least one third of his colleagues during his career were from Africa, South America, or Asia. All of them devoted to this club or that, their very emotions rattled with each team's weekly results. He was always curious as to how could such a simple game ignite that kind of passionate flame, but the boys seemed to love it and Robert was happy to see the family's athletic lineage being passed down. Matty rounded his younger brother, then fired a low drive past the small plastic goal. The misplaced shot allowed the ball roll to his grandfather. Robert did a quick hop stop as he settled the ball with the right instep of his shoe, spilling a bit of ale with the motion. The boy's laughter at pop pop's spilled drink was interrupted by a vile screech.

"Dinner is ready, let's go," Sasha squealed from the other side of the lawn, where the Robinson's massive deck met the makeshift pitch. Robert lined the bitch up, took two steps back, and launched a leather rocket toward his daughter in law. The flying ball, hit with furious pace, smashed square into Sasha's nose. Thick red liquid burst from her nostrils, cascaded down to her lips, fell to her chin, and dripped onto her very expensive white blouse. Eyes wide, mouth forming a wide smirk, Robert began a thunderous laughing fit until he noticed two little brown heads swarming at the feet of their mother. Matty and Marco were lapping up the fresh blood which dripped off of a tight pair of designer jeans and puddled around Momma's sneakers. Robert attempted to drive his grandson's away from the naughty nectar, but his words were washed away in the wind and his feet were frozen in fear. Matty turned to pop pop, giving him a red stained gleeful grin, his forehead slightly bulging through a crop of cute curly brown hair. Two small toothed knives replaced his perfect ivory incisors. The brothers faced each other, giggled, then leapt with unnatural ability toward their mother's throat. With her lower face drenched in a cascade of crimson, Sasha caught and cradled her baby boys as they latched to her wanting neck. As a geyser of red sprouted from the woman's new wounds, all three fell gracefully backwards onto the perfectly trimmed lawn.

Through swollen, sore, eyelids, Robert saw the steady spin of a dusty ceiling fan that methodically thumped with each passing.

"Well. Well. Well. Look who is finally coming to," A voice whispered from the right.

Robert cranked his neck and saw the gigantic dark man sitting on a cheap full-sized bed. The room was dim, but the man was darker than the night itself. Long dreadlocks parted perfectly from the top of the dark man's head, appearing to slither gracefully down past his massive shoulders. The dark man was topless but wore tight black athletic sweatpants which bulged at thigh and calf, coming to a rest just over a pair of all black high tops. With a perfectly chiseled face, anvils for arms, and a mid-section frame that would make any heavy weight jealous, Robert quickly concluded that the dark man must be the angel of death himself. Robert turned over again, eyes closed, awaiting another blow from the avenging evil angel.

"Nah, nah son, sit on up and take a drink," The dark man instructed.

Robert gently swung his stiff legs over the side of the bed, feeling every bit the age of seventy for the first time in weeks. He took the plastic cup from the daunting dark figure. A quick glance inside revealed more thick dark liquid. A squeamish grimace broke over his face, in response, the dark man laughed loudly.

"Now the sight of the shit makes you sick. Drink quick you blood thirsty bitch, we got a lot to cover," The dark man instructed through his dissipating laughter.

Robert held the plastic rim to his mouth, allowing the thick red fluid to fall over his tongue. Warm heat flowed down his throat, filling his undead tummy. This blood held the taste of strength, knowledge, and power. Cup emptied, Robert's life essence and physical stature returned nearly instantaneously, he felt dead alive again.

"My shit's nice, isn't it?" the dark man said, with a large smile and bobbing head accompanying his question.

"Who are you?" Robert questioned.

"For now, call me Roldi. And I am the mean motor scooter who saved your pasty pale dead ass," The dark man explained.

Robert cleared his eyes with human hands. He gave his head a few shakes, attempting to physically shrug off the cobwebs, the slight headache, and return to some semblance of reality. Whatever that was anymore, he thought before starting again.

"Did Katie send you?"

"She did," The dark man solemnly answered.

"Where is she?" Robert questioned.

"Dead," The dark man stated. The dark man begun again as he watched Robert's black pupils expand.

"Look son, we don't have a lot of time. I nearly took your damn head off. In fact, I should have taken your damn head off. Just chill a bit and let me explain," The dark man said, with imposing force, his words and tone taking a sinister turn. Robert felt true fear in his dead bones, he nodded accordingly and listened intently.

"Katie fucked up. Katie fucked up really good this time. Her and I have been together, undead brother and sister, for nearly three decades. I loved her more than you could ever know. Well maybe you do know, she told me about you and your wife. She told me what a good man you were. And I do mean were. But shit, this blessing can turn a gentle being into a maniacal monster right quick. Katie was only supposed to turn one person and even that was a complete fuck up. But my girl had an undead heart of rose gold. I tried to warn her, I tried man. Dammit. Anyway, let's get back on track. I'm not sure of how much she told you, but the man who made her and I, Marcel, was called to the head of our little tribe. He gave us both permission to start a nest, train together, then meet back up with him in a year or so. I saw it day one. Katie always wanted her own family, always wanted kids. So, she plucked two bad birds for her nest. Depressed, suicidal, or not, she should have never turned you Bob. There are no records in our kind's long history of anyone of your mortal age being turned. And Katie and I are still small children relatively speaking. As for her other new born bitten. Well, a sad case of a young woman with a terminal illness. Another big no no in the vampire bible. Some shit about cancer cells and reconstructed molecules driving a vamp crazy. You would know more about that kind of shit than me," The dark man explained. Robert was listening with intense concentration, but the dark man noticed his new roommate's eyes fluttering a bit. Robert was about to pass out again. "Damn, you need more rest. Probably need to take another shot later. Let me spin this yarn a bit quicker. Katie kept me in the loop. As an older vampire with a bit more patience, I wanted to take my time before I made my own immortal family. The young woman she turned went bat shit quick. Turning more into a feral animal than a civilized monster. After a few months, Katie thought she had her under control, then she found out about your wife. My sister always kept tabs on the few great humans she had met over time. You were always at the top of that list. I told her ass to leave you be, but she just wanted to check on you. Bob, you must have looked like one morose fuck, because she begged me to watch her psycho vamp daughter while she plotted your turn. By the time I got to New York, that freak had killed a couple homeless guys and a bartender. The nature of their deaths sent signals to those who hunt us. I will get to that later. I sent for Katie to return. The vamp freak had gone full on mad. A day. Two days. By the third day, I had to put her down. I nearly had to put your ass down as well. After a week and no Katie, I went looking for my little sister. I found baby girl's decapitated head sitting on a dresser at one of our safe houses. The motherfuckers didn't even have the place staked out, which means they are just fucking with us now. I thought maybe I could track you and get the bitches that did this. I arrived just in time to watch you get soaked in a blood bath. What a fucking month!" the dark man explained, letting out another laughing fit, which was a feeble attempt to mask his misery. Robert's eyes leaked red fluid from the terror tale. Feeling woozy again, he laid flat back on the bed and spoke. "Why didn't you kill me?" Robert asked.

"Two reasons. One. Our numbers are way down. Way down my ass, if Marcel was called to council, it means we are just about extinct. Two. The way Katie would talk about you, it would have been a sin to not try and get you under control. But trust me Bobby boy, you act the fool one hot second and I'll end your ass," The dark man responded.

"Where are we? And how long have I been out?" Robert whispered as he started to fade to black again.

"Outside of Pittsburg. You been out about two days. Yeah, sorry about that, I slapped your ass a bit too hard. Thought all the blood you took in would have had you geared to take the strike, but damn I'm strong son," The dark man answered.

"My son. I have to contact my son," Robert whispered, the words now barely floating out of his mouth, a mortal man would not have been able to make out the mutter, but Roldi's heightened hearing heard him fine.

"We will handle that in time. Don't know how much you remember Bob, but you took out a few old ladies and a high-ranking lawman. I'm fairly sure from the tidbits of news from that night, that you chomped up three others outside of some shit motel. All the scanners and media reports have said not a damn thing about you, which means a federal level search is on for your ass now, which also means our enemies know what the fuck you are. I torched the place and swiped clear the cheap ass security system. I give us about five days until we are chopped up or staked down," The dark man explained.

"I have to, have to, call my son," Robert said, the words now barely audible even to supernatural ears.

"You don't have to do anything right now but stay undead and live," The dark man said.

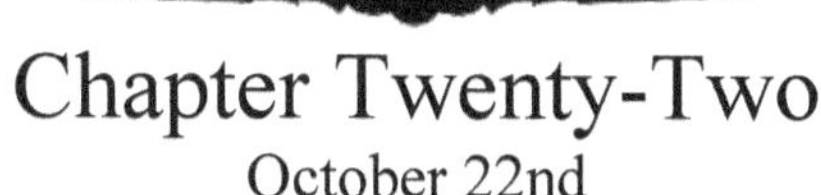

Chapter Twenty-Two
October 22nd

Walking around the expansive sitting room, Ronson craved a smoke. How much of this furniture cost more than his car he silently thought to himself? The home was impressive but reeked of sadness and despair. How could it not? A dead wife and mother coupled with a missing father and grandfather, who is now a serious suspect, caused an awful aromatic atmosphere to swirl of off the high vaulted ceilings. Shockingly, the lord of the manner was holding it together with courageous demeanor. Shaken yes, but Matthew Robinson gave the perception of being relieved of his wife's demise and only concerned with the whereabouts of his father. The detective could hear the good doctor concluding another serious phone call in his designer kitchen. Ronson was eager to have a one on one with the man. Matthew walked into the room with the confidence of a highly successful man along with the determination of someone who wanted more finite answers. Matthew started with an apology.

"Detective Ronson, sorry for the delay. My kids are at their aunt's house, Sasha's sister. My oldest is starting to realize that his mother is not coming home. We have tried to keep it all in check, but I am afraid I am going to have a tough conversation with my sons tonight. Can I get you something to drink?" Ronson declined. Then took an offered seat directly across from his host.

"I have been at this a long time Doctor Robinson. The aftermath and explanations are often worse than the horrors of the incidents themselves," Ronson explained. Matthew nodded then asked the detective to please call him Matt. Ronson nodded and offered to be addressed by his first name as well. The two agreed, to the joy of Ronson. Most upper-class citizens demanded their titles be spoken, as if addressing a proper lord. Formalizing the conversation always helped in gaining pertinent information. Ronson began again. "Matt, I am here to help in anyway. I promise to shoot straight with you despite some hard news. I will answer any questions you have. If I do not have the answers, I will move heaven and earth to try and get them for you."

"I appreciate that Billy and all of the support your department has given so far. As you may know, I have hired a personal team to investigate, but in no way, shape, or form, will they interfere with your investigation," Matt responded, with the determination that suited his professional stature.

"I understand. If it pleases you, I would like to question first. Then answer anything I can for you," Ronson explained. Doctor Robinson agreed and the difficult inquisition began.

"Did you at any time think that your wife might be seeing another man?" Ronson asked.

"Yes, she fucked many other men during our marriage. I always knew, but we kind of swept it under the rug. We had an informal agreement. No questions asked, no lies to tell. I would like for us to be deadly honest detective, so I will let you know that I to have had a few affairs. I am currently in a physical only relationship with a nurse at my job," Matthew boldly responded. Ronson was a bit taken back, yet admired the man's honesty.

"It is a difficult situation all the way round, I appreciate your honest response. Would your father have any reason to attack or harm your wife? Would he have suspected her indiscretions?" Ronson asked.

"Both of my parents never liked her from the jump. They had true love and no concept of the mayhem of modern-day relationships. I mean, today, marriage is more of an economical arrangement and task mastering than spending a lifetime with your soul mate. It's sad but true, especially in the high-end world of societal status." Ronson nodded, then continued,

"I know nothing of that world either, nor have I ever been married. A lawman's life is tough on relationships. One in every three law enforcement marriages end in divorce. But I will digress. Matt. As you know, we have no idea where your father is. Making him a suspect in both the murder of your wife, two other victims, and the tragedy at The Shores. Between me, you, and the fencepost, we have no other suspects. No evidence of any kind and only pulled in a few foul bikers that were at the motel that night. None of which possess the kind of physical prowess to commit the crimes found in and around the river."

"Physical prowess?" Matt asked.

Ronson took a deep breath, preparing himself for the explanation. "Well, one victim's skull was crushed on some rocks. Another's had their genitalia torn straight off of their body. I know you have examined the report on your wife. So, the black bear theory that seems to be the popular explanation is out of the window, unless the bear chased the three to the river, gave Mrs. Robinson a deadly love bite, swiped a man's cock off and then bashed the other man's head on some rocks. And concluded by gently placing the man half in and out of the water. Add to that, no hint of large animal tracks, and we have ourselves a very human murder investigation. Is there any reason to believe you father found out about your wife's affair and hired some very large men to take care of her and her lover?" Matt still seemed amused at the thought of Sasha's lover having his cock torn off, his serious demeanor lightened for a moment before he spoke.

"Not a chance. My father never liked her, may have actually suspected her of running around, but never in a million years could I believe my father to do something like that."

"Your father was a loved and highly respected man. Last question Matt. Did you notice anything different about your father over the last couple weeks? His general mode or appearance?" Ronson questioned.

"Nothing at all to be honest," Matt responded, lying for the first time. Ronson noticed with ease.

"Well Matt, right now this is all we have. A black bear theory and some sick arsonist that struck and snuck away into the night. Thank you for your help. Now if you have any questions, shoot," Ronson said, a little miffed that the man he was empathizing with had seemed to turn coat quickly, adding to the mystery around Robert Robinson. Also burdened that he would now have to dig into Matthew's life as the two may have been in on the crimes.

"Just a one. Do you have any idea where my father is?" Matthew asked. Pleasing to Ronson as the detective knew now that this man was not only not involved in this mess, but he truly did not have any clue to where his father was.

"Dead honest Matt. I have no clue. His apartment was torched. The bodies are all identified. No one he associated with has any clue, nor did they speak to him on the nineteenth. The cell company has no records of any conversations from that night. Only calls from you the last two days and some kid named Bruce. His financial accounts have no activity and his car was left at the community. It is at the impound now, we are through with it, you can pick it up anytime you get a chance. Matt, this is the coldest of cold cases, but in the end, even glaciers thaw," Ronson explained.

The detective and the doctor shook hands admirably as parted company. Matthew began preparations to cash in every favor owed to him and there were many. Billy prepared to start a solo man hunt for the person he believed killed his partner.

Entering a dive bar called the Rebel Yell was intimidating enough. Entering with a six-foot-six black man was another level all together. The denim clad crowd mugged the odd couple with eyes that were as welcoming as a Serbian hit squad. An hour earlier Robert woke after another day long slumber, this time feeling fully refreshed. Ready to launch a barrage of questions at his new best friend, Roldi handed him some thrift store sweats and told him to wash up, they were heading out for a bit. Not wanting to offend the dark man, who looked even larger as they stood side by side, Robert took an ice-cold shower, then threw on the humble attire. Both undead men sat at a cramped booth at the end of the bar. The torn red cushioned benches were surprising soft. The humble wooden table attached to the wall would have been a bit more rustically charming if not for the confederate flag that hung above it.

"What the fuck are we doing here?" Robert asked.

"Shhhhhh. Damn man, not so loud. We can speak soft as shit and hear each other you dumb ass infant," Roldi answered. Then begun again.

"I've been coming here for decades. They stare down anyone they don't know. Got a meth lab in the basement of this place. They could care less that I'm black or that you look like some yuppie with poor fashion sense. They are just making sure we're not the law."

A young woman that looked ten years older than she should arrived at the end of Roldi's statement. The older, darker vampire ordered up a numbered meal before the server could even present them with sticky menus. She took the order, gave a yellow toothed smile, then returned quickly with a domestic beer for Robert and a rum and coke for Roldi. The atmosphere lightened as the waitress was pleased with the knowledge that the black man must have been here before with his knowledge of their menu. Her pleasant manner gave signal to the rest of the bar that the two strangers were on the level. Roldi flashed her a Colgate clean smile as she told them that the grill was a little overloaded and their order would take longer than expected. Both undead dudes stated that there was no rush.

"I'm guessing we always give the illusion of eating and drinking when out in public?" Robert asked.

"Lord almighty, of course man. Katie rushed your damn ass so fast. Look, you can still enjoy a drink and food, just some tricks to it. Watch," Roldi explained.

The dark man glanced around to make sure no one was still giving the odd couple, the jail yard stare. With the kind of speed that only Robert could catch, Roldi sliced his thumb with pointer finger and squeezed a few droplets into his tall glass of cola and sweet liquor. The tall glass gave the illusion of a shot glass as Roldi held it to his thick purple lips and sipped.

"Yummmmy rummmmy. Just a little squeeze into your drink or onto food and it almost taste like it did when you were a mortal," Roldi explained. He gestured with a nod to Robert, signaling the infant vampire to try it.

Not yet possessing the talent and speed of the more experienced creature, Robert made a larger than expected gash on his thumb, clumsily splashing a steady drip of blood into the small bottle head, as wells as getting a good portion on the table as well. Roldi laughed as one would watching a baby try to inhale their first bite from a spoon.

"Ah shit, this gonna be real fun," Roldi said, and then continued,

"Look brother, I know this has been one weird trip, but we are almost home free. So, here's the news. While you were still recovering from my right cross, I got the scoop. As per the media outlets, the fire at your place was a freak accident. You are gonna love this. The three people you drained dry, the puppets on TV are calling it a freak bear attack. This means everything is officially signed sealed and delivered to the church," Roldi explained.

"The church? What the hell does the church have to do with arson and murder?" Robert questioned.

"Would you lower your fucking voice! For the second fucking time, we just have to whisper dumbass," Roldi said. Robert finally got it as he noticed that the dark man's lips barely moved when he spoke. The patrons probably noticed two weirdos staring at each other, not speaking at all.

"We ain't gonna make it you keep flapping your fanged up dentures old man. Now just fucking listen. Hold up," Roldi said, then rubbed his hands together and flashed another fangless smile to the server. She placed an order of honey wings in front of Roldi. A fat cheeseburger in front of Robert. They saw her off without a next round of drink order. In unnatural speed, Roldi opened a new thumbed wound and dosed his wings with red sauce. After taking down two wings, Roldi began again, "The church has been hunting our kind since the beginning. It's a long ass tale for another damn time, but here is the broad strokes. Not even Marcel knows the true origins, but the fairy tale speaks of five priest that contracted the Bubonic plague in 1347. These priest all came from the same town in Bucharest and shared a blood line. Allegedly, the virus mutated them and when they started to grow fangs, feast on sheep, and weaken in the sun, they were sent to Pope Clement. When they got to the holy land, a guard of his holiness slit one of the priest arms and watched the wound heal nearly instantaneously. Clement told them that the lord had blessed them, and promised that he would share their blood with the world. Of course, like most pious pricks, he was to have them burned in their rooms the next day. Father Darius tried to warn his brothers that he could sense that the pope was full of shit and meant to kill them. Darius escaped in the night while the other four were torched in their sleep. Darius learned the art of turning over time, fast forward about three hundred years later, Darius formed a small army which helped the Ottomans fight the church. Darius was beheaded in battle and the remnants of his dark blood line set up permanent camp in and around Transylvania, protected by the shadow of the Carpathians. The church formed a sect to rid the world of blood suckers and this and that happened and here we are, two assholes having burgers and wings." Roldi finished by lifting a meaty wing in mocking fashion. A lover of history, Robert was fascinated with the tale, desperately eager to fill in the blanks.

"So, did one of Darius's children actually bite Vlad the Impaler? And how did vampires make it here?" Robert eagerly asked.

"Man, once we are up north you can sit your happy ass down and find out. But for now, listen the fuck up. The good news is your face is not all over the internet or TV as America's most wanted. And by the grace of Darius himself, we made it out without being tracked. They caught up to Katie somewhere between your spot and a safe house in Philly. Baby girl somehow covered her tracks to you, but these fucks got satellites, military consultants in every damn region, and they will be relentlessly hunting you until your head is off or heart pierced by a fancy ass silver sword. Now, my boy got the coast clear for us to make it to him tomorrow night. We just got to eat up, lay low, then we are half way home. Once we get to where we got to be, I promise we will get word out to your son without getting him involved. And for fucks sake don't bite anyone when you're out on a walk later," Roldi said.

"Walk later?" Robert asked.

"Yeah, your ass is going for a nice long walk while I entertain my company," Roldi explained. The dark man shot a glance over to the server, she returned his gaze with a blush and a giggle.

"Do you really think that's a good idea right now?" Robert asked. "Look man, blood is blood, but pussy is pussy," Roldi clarified with authority.

⬥

Chapter Twenty-Three
October 23rd

Hour two and the fourth lap around the motel, the server's moans could still be heard. No supernatural sonar was needed to hear her love sonnet. Robert let out a sigh, then headed back toward the wooded area for another walk in the brush. Since they got back to the hotel, his mind had been on the dark history of his new kind. At least once a week during his mortal life, Robert would binge watch history shows, fascinated with the tales of war and heroism. His imagination ran rampant with thoughts of how vampires have shaped history. Questions and the allure of the subject matter was a welcomed relief from the horrors of the last month. Thoughts turned to why so many of these shit ass motels were built around thick woods when he heard the waitress's giggles and Roldi's well wishes as he sent her off into the night. Flushed with passion and decked in quickly thrown on unbuttoned jeans and untucked employee polo, the server hoped in her old Mustang. She speed off with a world class erotic tale to tell.

"Hustle up buttercup," Roldi shouted to Robert, before quickly disappeared behind the open door to their room.

A blinding black tornado whipped across the room as Robert entered. Roldi was straighten up, quickly loading clothes. He put what looked like two smaller hand guns into a large gym bag. The speed at which the older vampire moved was mesmerizing to Robert. Tossing the bag to his ward, Roldi laid out the plan.

"Alright son, hold on to that. I'm going to do a quick go around the property, leave some cash in the drop box. When I honk the horn, move your dead ass. Got it?" Robert nodded.

About three minutes later the honk came. Robert sprinted to the black-on-black large SUV. The two undead men speed off into the fall night. Loud rap music rolled out of the vehicle's speakers, the lyrics and artist unknown to Robert, he gazed over to Roldi, who's eyes were darting back and forth as he drove.

"Where are we headed?" Robert questioned loudly to be heard over the rhythmic tunes.

"North," Roldi responded, eyes still scanning the surrounding area, as if looking for a galloping deer to spring out at any moment.

The narrow road opened to a four-lane highway. The heavy brush that surrounded them appeared to clear. Robert glanced to the side and saw small strip malls and quite neighborhoods emerge. The site of civilization seemed to put the dark old vampire at ease. Roldi flicked his thumb on the volume button on the steering wheel, in response, silence surrounded the two riders.

"Here's the news. We are going to see my boy, Jerry. Oh, you are gonna love old Jerry. We wait at his spot till I get word from Marcel and then we are headed to one artic ass location," Roldi explained.

"How long to we get to Jerry?" Robert questioned.

"Bout two hours. Should get there with plenty of darkness left before dawn," Roldi replied.

"Where is the artic ass location?" Robert asked.

"Damn man, chill with the fifty questions. Let's get to my boy's spot first. Then we go from there. Fuck me you are one annoying ass bitch, spending eternity with you is gonna be fucking torturous," Roldi replied.

Robert crossed his arms as he took in the speeding sights from his passenger side window in complete silence. A half hour flew by before Roldi took an exit that led into Ohio. A few minutes later they were once again cruising down a two-lane hidden road that was surrounded by the casting shadows of a tree covered mountainous region.

"You gonna mope the rest of the way or what son?" Roldi questioned after the long silence.

"Well, I have to wait for answers as always, so what's the point?" Robert answered.

"You are one prissy bitch, you know that right?" Roldi responded with a laugh. The laugh broke up the silent standoff. Roldi started again. "Alright, go ahead, shot a question."

"So how did you become a vampire?" Robert asked.

"Well, now we are getting to know each other. I was born Roland Burton in 1956, reborn Roldilockz in 1972, then reborn again in 1974. My pops was a janitor in Brooklyn for apartment complexes and my mom, well momma was a Jamaican immigrant that cleaned houses. I had two older brothers, all three of us took after mom. Followed her passion for music. Rap actually started at street parties in Brooklyn. I had a very unique talent for stringing rhyming words together with ease. Mom's old British lingo combined with the slang on the streets gave me a linguistic advantage to spit out lyrics like a rapid mouthed African Grey. Disco was popping but my brothers saw rap was the future, they had me performing in Central Park every weekend. When I turned sixteen most of the city came to see Roldilockz sing by the carousel every Saturday evening. Got my name because of my darling dreads. Two months before heading to NYU on a full artist scholarship, I had a performance in the park. I always stuck around after to chat up the crowd. Always looking for a bell-bottomed beauty to take a long walk with and steal a kiss under the New York night. A rainstorm cleared out the crowd early. I took cover under a large Hackberry tree. They were always good for shade in the summer. About thirty yards away the carousel lights came on and the child's ride started to spin at an unusual speed. Flashing around about every ten seconds was a tall pale man. Now Bob, I'm straight as an arrow but this moutherfucker looked like he walked right off an Italian runway. You can't believe me until you meet the man. I was memorized by him. As the ride spun faster, he appeared to be floating toward me, the rain only enhanced his beauty. A mystical figure illuminated by the sparkle of tears from the heavens. His black eyes met my brown pupils, putting me in a beautiful terror trance. Funny shit, it was like I completely wanted him to bite me. Marcel gently turned me. Long ass story short. The first month was rough. I missed the shit out of my family. The beautiful immortal man had to subdue me several times. We fabricated a story to my family that I ran off with a man. My father, an old school southerner, disowned me, but mom and my brothers kept in touch. After Marcel got me fully trained, I would see them time and again. Much more after pops passed. My oldest brother, Mikey, he's still around. I send money to my nieces and nephews. Getting harder to visit as I have to completely do a six-hour makeover to look my mortal age."

A pause fell over the two after Roldi concluded, then Robert started again,

"So why did Marcel turn you?"

"He loves beauty. Marcel is three hundred years or some shit old. He said I had the most exotically beautiful voice that ever entered his ears. And Katie, well, damn man you know. She had to be the most stunning woman I've ever seen. And those tits…" BOOOOOOOMMMMMMMMM.

Robert's fingernails and fangs popped at impact, an auto defensive system, triggered by innate fear of harm. The SUV did a complete three sixty and accelerated through a guardrail on the opposite lane from which they were driving. Roldi was already five feet deep in the woods when he yelped. "Move Bob!" Robert hurtled the center consul, his nails slicing through the driver's side leather seat as he catapulted toward his new dark friend. Roldi took off into the darkness. Robert followed as fast as he could, trying to keep pace with the sight of the bouncing dreads in front of him. Shots rang out like rapid fire firecrackers. Steam erupted out over Roldi's left shoulder. The dark man turned shouted.

"Bob, get behind that tree quick, kill any fucking thing that comes this way," Roldi instructed, then scaled a massive tree like a giant black squirrel. Robert stood behind a large oak. The sound of the woodland creatures scurrying from the scene was only interrupted by the quick approach of their assailants. Quick but careful, the attackers came at them with deadly desire.

"Mostrarse a si mismo putas no-muertos!" One of the attackers screeched.

Feeling full fear for the first time since being turned, Robert's emotion switched to quick curiosity. Stunned that the voice was speaking Spanish. More stunned that it had come from female vocal cords. A loud thump crushed the bark on the front side of the tree he was hiding behind, followed by a war cry from above. Roldi leapt from a sturdy branch, landing on top of an olive-skinned woman. In a flash he twisted her neck with force, snapping it as a child would a twig. The crack of her spine and the sight of her head leaving the torso caused Robert to gag. Shots rang out again, a few hit Roldi, his skin exploded with more steam. White mist appeared to burst from his wounds as the dark man roared into the night. More Spanish alleged vulgarity rang though the night. The second attacker appeared around the clearing thirty yards from Robert's hiding spot. The site of her fallen friend sent the woman into a shooting frenzy, the automatic weapons, one in each hand, spat tiny torpedoes all through the forest. Several shattering Robert's tree fortress. A brief silence after the shooting spree and a crunch instead of a crack burst through the woods. Robert peered from the left of the oak and saw that Roldi had circled behind the woman. The dark man nearly bit half of her throat off as he chomped on her neck. A few moments later, the dark man tossed the tanned corpse against a tree like a child would dismiss an old rag doll.

"Stay put!" Roldi commanded. Robert shook his head as he coward again behind his hiding spot. Ears perked for any new attacks. A minute later Roldi burst to his side, and warm red piss flowed down Robert's leg from the pure startling shock of his friend's unannounced arrival. White steam still seeped from the dark man.

"You alright man?" Roldi questioned.

"Yeah, are you?" Robert responded.

"I'll die to die another day," Roldi answered.

His choice of words plastered a curious look on Robert's face but helped him to snap back to reality.

"Who the fuck were they?" Robert asked, still slightly shaken.

"Nuns," Roldi explained, still shooting glances through the darkness.

"Nuns?" Robert asked again.

"Yeah motherfucker, Nuns," Roldi explained again.

Still in disbelief, Robert fished again. "Like Nun Nuns?"

"YES! Like don't want Nun. Can't have Nun. Ruler wielding, bad bitches of Christ. Nuns!" Roldi shouted. Putting an end to the examination.

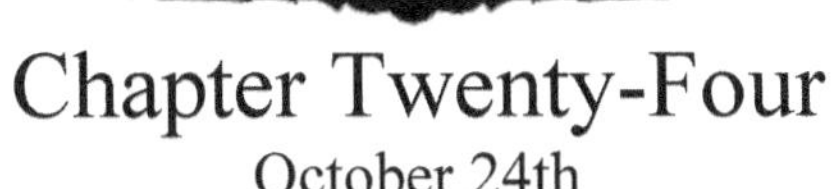

Chapter Twenty-Four
October 24th

Clattering of fingers against keyboards and curse filled jokes echoed through the police station and into the boss man's office. Quickly silenced as Commander Muller shut the tinted glass door. The large man rounded Ronson to take a seat behind his elaborate hand carved wooden desk. Chomping at the bit with information, Ronson started to squeal,

"Boss you are not going to believe some of this shit."

Muller leaned back, closed his eyes, and shook his head, a nod to let his detective explain. Ronson continued,

"I went back to the place Robinson worked. Been at this a long-time boss, I can still be fooled, but this woman described in crazy detail and with the conviction of someone who was being water boarded, that Robinson turned into some kind of creature. I pulled the security footage, but it was too blurry to make out. The other woman, the manager I think, shows me footage of the man tossing a cart like a stone with one swipe of his hand. Some delivery company reported him to the store's corporate office. Both ladies said Starkes was asking the same questions the same day of the fire. Then, I go to see this Bruce kid and his boyfriend, you gotta see this piece of work, starts in with the same tall tale. Robinson came over, leapt at him in some crazy animal way. Kid says Robinson's face was contorted. He swears the old man had fangs for teeth and claws for nails. Except for the kid having a minor possession charge, neither him nor the woman have any sort of record at all. O.K, I tell myself, they all are a little low brow. They all know each other, so I keep digging. Robinson calls the victim Sasha, his daughter in law, around about the day before the murders. I got the recording. The way he is leading her in the conversation, he was obviously fishing. Robinson knew she was running around and wanted to catch her. Phone company said Starkes pulled the conversation as well. Our man was all over this. I have to guess, the old man got into some heavy drugs with the dead drowned guy, then went batshit. He's definitely responsible for this. Now Wilkens calls me. Says that some girl that Robinson hooked up with wants to talk to us. Hooked up? Christ, this old bastard has really started living at seventy. I'm meeting with her around three, but we have got to get the word to federal and state. Not one dollar or cent has been withdrawn from his account. No one, and I mean no one, has any clue to where he might have gone. His son has put a team together, some local mercs, to find him. I was at the academy with the guy leading doctor Robinson's band of misfit men. He's an old school Navy guy, he tells me the son doesn't have a fucking clue to where his father is. They are starting down south where the old man still had some old friends. How the hell this man has escaped so fast, without cash or a car, has me baffled. But we will get him, we must, for Starkes."

The captain leaned back, lips pursed as he broke the news quietly, with fear of an overly emotion reaction from his detective. "Billy, when you go for it, there is really no one better. I know you admired Starkes, shit, we all did. He was a giant amongst ants. Look Billy, this is going to be tough, but hear me out. You got eleven weeks left. With all admiration and sincerity, I am ordering you to let this one go."

Ronson pulled a funny face, quickly replaced with an angry inquisitive one. "Let it go? As in, I'm off the case?"

Mueller explained, "Starkes was just passing by brother, we all knew that. And he was consulting with departments that I have never even heard of. Those people are all over this. I repeat. Let it go."

Ronson wanted to scream. Ronson wanted to shout. Ronson wanted a good god damn explanation. But the boss had always had his back. The boss backed off when he knew that his detective was done hustling years ago. The boss stood up for him when he fucked up the evidence on a major drug bust. Ronson stood slowly and nodded to the captain. Mueller gave him some final encouragement and instruction.

"He was a great man. Billy, you are a great man. We all have lost brothers over the years. This is nothing new. His ghost will circle you for weeks, pop up on occasion for months, then fly away with the others within a year. No need right now to partner you up so close to the end. So just take a seat on the bench till the whistle blows, then try like hell to enjoy yourself. Understood?" Ronson gave a fake smile, nodded again, and headed to his desk. The incessant noise from the office did nothing to alleviate the shock of his dismissal orders. Billy opened the top cabinet of his metal desk and popped two Tylenol like PEZ. Mueller was serious, that was what scared him the most. Even when the feds came in, they always welcomed help from the department. How high the fuck up was Starkes? What in the hell are they worried about? Billy wanted justice for his friend, he also feared that this old man gone wild was going to kill again. A yellow sticky note attached to the bottom of his computer screen waved back and forth from the wind coming in through the open window in front of his desk. A number with the words, Luna: Starkes Case, was scribbled on the it. Ronson tore the paper off with force, crumpled it forcefully into a ball and tossed it in the plastic bin. He knew Starkes had talked to her too. Too dangerous to meet with as they, whoever the hell they were, would know if he questioned her. Nope, not today Satan. Ronson was not going to sit the last dance out, but he was not going to force himself on the prom queen either. He would waltz in the shadows, alone, until this was over, until the last record stopped spinning.

Clawing sounds rumbled from above, then a speck of dawn shot down through the dark dirt. More tiny holes followed shortly after Roldi dusted the soil off of Robert's pale face.

"Evening sunshine, how was your first dirt nap?" Roldi questioned. His pleasant demeanor and wide smile alleviated some of the anxiety from the previous night. Roldi assisted the new vampire from his earth-bound bed.

"Didn't sleep a wink, but thanks for asking," Robert replied, as he attempted to push himself back to the grassy surface.

"First time going to ground is tough enough. Under last night's circumstances is another story. I'm proud of you son. Eat some breakfast, it will perk you up," Roldi said. He pointed to the near lifeless deer. Robert strolled over and bent down next to the beautiful white tail. The animal's labored breathing and sad eyes made it hard for the empathic vampire to bring on the change.

"Ahhhh, for fucks sake," Roldi said, then pushed the newbie vamp out of the way. With the ruthless touch of an executioner, Roldi slit the deer's furry neck. Rich red blood poured from the wound. The site of nature's death nectar caused Robert's fangs to pop so fast, they punctured his lower lip. On bended knee he slurped the flowing wild wine with fever. Katie nailed it. A fresh doe tasted a hundred times better than any ale he had ever downed. The forest seemed to erupt around him. The owl's hoots sounded like trumpets from heaven. The scattering of foxes in the brush were as clear as a buffalo herd stamping through a field. Filled and feisty, Robert stood and let out a loud blood burb.

"Damn you crude bitch," Roldi said.

"Sorry. Man, that was incredible," Robert explained.

"Wait till you taste a tiger. That shit is like crack on a porterhouse."

Robert contemplated the statement, let it slide for another time and asked the obvious,

"Where the hell are we? What do we do now?"

"Well, good news, bad news. Good news, that was just a scout team. If it were a seminary squad, our heads would be on branches right now. My guess, they sent scout squads in each direction from your old folks home. Bad news, we are gonna have to hike it from here. Too dangerous to grab a vehicle. The traffic cams will pick us up right quick," Roldi explained.

"How far away are we from where we have to go?"

"Well, we are around Youngstown now, so about ninety miles."

"Ninety miles! That will take a week if we're lucky."

"You are the dumbest fucking smart guy I've met. You think we are going for a brisk walk in the woods asshole? We are headed on a night jog. Even if I slow down for your old ass, we can get there in about three hours. Been to old Jerry's a dozen times. We will be covered most of the way through the shade of the forest that runs all through RT. 80," Roldi explained. Robert quickly remembered his newfound gift of speed. Robert pestered the older vampire with another question.

"What if the Nuns show up again?"

"We run faster and lead them away from Jerry. I buried those bitches deep, but since they probably needed to check in, I say we still got about a good five minutes before their crew know they are gone. Nuns can hunt for days on end, but usually check in at least every twenty-four hours," Roldi explained.

"Five minutes?" Robert questioned.

"Yeah, so keep up son," Roldi stated, then took off north through the quickly darkening night.

Robert kicked his legs in gear in pursuit of the dark man. Afraid that he was not good enough, Robert trained like a mad man before his freshmen year of college. During the first week of winter work outs, he was in the best shape of his life. During warm up sprints, his legs felt light as a feather as he glided past his teammates during fitness drills. Seemingly skipping over the frosted grass. This night run was a thousand times more intense and enjoyable. No pain, no labored breathing, just pure energetic ecstasy. Woodland creatures scattered, flew, and crawled quickly away from the predators that passed quickly through their orange leafed littered kingdom. After a few minutes, the motion of running kicked into auto gear. The entire last couple of days swarmed like a dark horde of wasp through Robert's thoughts. Thunderbolts of questions and anticipation struck through his undead synapsis like a jackhammer hitting concrete. How was his son and grandkids doing? Did they think or know that he had killed their wife and mother? Would God forgive him for these sins? Was there a God? How could the government and church keep this dark secret in the modern world, where every person held a camera at their fingertips? Was this new dark life worth all of this horror and death? Roldi for some reason, probably out of loyalty to Katie, had protected him against the Nuns. But would he eventually turn on him if the chips were really down? Each self-examining question met with another, causing an eternal debate that would not be settled anytime soon. Roldi slowed in the distance and held his hand up. How long had they been running? Robert paused, awaiting his dark mentor's instructions. Glancing up, he saw a large old Ferris wheel in the distance accompanied with the sweet smell of the sea. Roldi turned and spoke softly, "Tread carefully, we are here."

Chapter Twenty-Five
October 25th

Ronson Slipped past the front desk clerk and office team in the front of the lobby with ease. All of them decked out in overly expensive attire that made their jobs look way more important than they actually were. Pinnacle Point, a luxury condominium community in downtown Baltimore, was where Starkes had called home for a little over a year. A smart looking part of town for a smart man. Starkes had given Ronson a key to his home the first day they met, unusual, but not uncommon for detectives. Billy had only been here once before. that was to pick up and scan some documents that his partner had left and needed while on one of many consulting cases with the feds. The elevator pinged and Ronson moved quickly to his dead friend's home. His worn Aldo's clicking loudly against the marble hallway flooring. Unit 5d sat at the end of the floor on the left. For the first time in years, the veteran detective's hand slightly trembled as he attempted to insert the key into the lock. Mueller's commanding order, with no real reason on resolve, to pull him so quickly off the case, had Billy rattled. A quick clicking sound brought some relief as he was sure that someone from somewhere higher up than he, or the owner of the unit, would have had the place scoped and locks changes already. Starkes's sister in Chicago had informed the department that she held all of his personal important belongings and to have anything left sent to charity. She had paid the termination fee on the lease and Ronson had found out that the unit was being listed for lease by owner by Thanksgiving. Another wave of relief hit as the a-type Starkes's home looked in the same pristine condition it had the first time Billy had been there. A simple one-bedroom floorplan that was blanketed with expensive looking granite countertops, high end appliances and eloquent furniture. Several minutes after snooping through the clueless kitchen and living room, Ronson made his way to his friend's bedroom. Next to the perfectly made bed sat a few odd books on a glass toped nightstand. John Marks's "Fangland" sat on top of Stoker's immortal classic, "Dracula," Ronson never took Starkes for a fiction reader, penciled him in as a history buff like the rest of the department boys. The bedroom held no other clues or hints as to what his partner was up to. Concluding his tour, Ronson parked his ass in the fine leather chair that sat in front of Starkes's small work desk, which housed a large monitor, standard keyboard, and printing machine. Unfortunately, no papers, folders, or notes were sprinkled on or around the work station. The detective's pudgy middle finger hit the enter button. He was a tad startled to see the screen pop to life. A refence page popped up. The header at the top of the search screen read: VAMPIRE LORE.

"Mister Ronson," a voice floated in through the living room, calm but commanding. Ronson nearly did a backflip off of the chair. The rattled detective reached for his revolver with voiced response.

"Yeah, who is it?"

"Friends of Mr. Starkes, we are unarmed and entering the bedroom please do not be alarmed," The voice responded.

Ronson held his pistol firm, knowing this must be either another law agent or someone involved in this odd case. How the hell did they know he was there? How could they see he had pulled his weapon, when the hallway was completely blocked off from the living room. Three men strolled confidently, with arms raised, into the large bedroom. Two were dressed in standard priest clothes, the third in more decorative religious attire.

"Mister Ronson, I am Bishop Lopez. I am pleased and thankful to meet you," The short bald man explained. Ronson stood and the two shook hands. Lopez walked slowly over to the edge of the king-sized bed and sat towards the intruder. The other two priests stood at sentinel attention to the left of the more distinguished holy man.

"I understood Mr. Starkes to have been a non-practicing Baptist. Was he not Bishop?" Ronson questioned.

"From my intel, that was the case Mr. Ronson," Lopez replied.

"So why is the Catholic Church here? Did ugh, his sister send you?" Ronson asked.

With all of his training and high cognitive intellect, Ronson could not for the life of him imagine why a high-ranking church official was at his partner's place. Ronson fully expected either the feds or some covert government agency to maybe pop in, but the church?

"Well Mr. Ronson, we have vested interest in some of Mr. Starkes's work. I do believe your superiors have told you that others would be taking over the tragedy that fell upon this great man," Lopez explained.

The stoic holy man slightly raised his voice when saying the word superiors, as if he himself had given the order.

"I'm not on any case, I just came to gather a few of my friend's belongings. To send to his family," Ronson said.

"Ah, Erica, his sister. We have sent her our condolences along with promises that we would pray day and night for a week for her brother to enter the Lord's kingdom," Lopez replied.

Around a decade ago, Ronson had the unfortunate task of taking on a case where the church had allegedly covered up for a big-time con artist that had ripped off thousands of seniors, but the scumbag was a massive donor to the man upstairs. Before any proper investigation could be conducted, most of the people got their money back, the case got shut down quickly, and the boss man explained that the men in robes could just about buy their way out of anything. Protecting those that kept the air conditioning running through the massive temples of worship. Ronson got the hint, shook the case off, and the result reaffirmed what he always thought about organized religion. Billy was about to give a sermon of his own to the bishop when the commander walked in the room.

"Billy. Everyone on the force would like to thank you for your many years of service It is my great honor to inform you that your request for retirement has been approved and expedited from January as to effective immediately. Please report to the department to turn in your badge and side arm. Your full pension and retirement benefits will begin next month," Mueller explained with more force than pride.

Ronson stared at the man he knew for over twenty years with disdain.

"Congratulations Mr. Ronson. Enjoy Florida. I spent many years in St. Augustine as a pastor," Lopez added.

Ronson wanted to choke the prick out but got the hint. Walking with defeated demeanor, the veteran detective walked past the decorated inhabitants of his friend's bedroom without words. Once inside his car, Ronson gave the steering wheel a punch, finally feeling free to let out some pent-up emotion. Cold fall air entered the

Ford as he pushed the tiny button to lower the window and lite up a smoke. What the hell the church had to do with all of this made his head spin. One long drag after another, the detective tried to inhale reason instead of nicotine. Just sign the papers, pack up and head south. An instant before saying fuck it, a loud clatter caught his attention. His eyes darted across the street. Two cyclists collided into each other and were helmet to helmet about to throw down. Quickly realizing it was no longer his problem, Billy was about to hit the start button to kick over the engine when he noticed the cartoon figure beyond the cyclist. A large muppet like vampire figure held two books in each hand, oddly enough inviting bystanders to enter the book store and take a bite out of books. Ronson put his smoke out in a half-filled plastic cup, then leaned his head on the top of the steering wheel. Vampire books, the Catholic church, Starkes's indented skull, Robinson's transformation. Disbelief became reality real quick. A lifetime of hunting human monsters and his end was brought about by a mythical one. He was looking forward to a mind numbing, relaxing, stress free retirement. Two last thoughts crossed his mind before he headed to turn in his badge. One. He could kiss relaxing goodbye until he got to the bottom of this. Two. At least he could conduct his own investigation under the bright protection of the sunshine state.

Chapter Twenty-Six
October 26th

Jerry Jenkins was both a blessing and a nightmare for Robert. Katie was stunning, Roldi was a walking talking dark demi-god, Jerry just about looked like every accountant Robert had ever seen in the cardiac ward. Barely five foot five, skin paler than a milky full moon, and shockingly at least thirty pounds overweight. His physical appearance eliminated the notion that all vampires were gorgeous lords of the night. Roldi explained to Robert that the change affected everyone differently. That undead blood was magical but there was no cure for ugly. Forty-eight hours after meeting his third vampire, Robert hid in the back of the library, pretending to glance at political books just to get some reprieve from his newest friend. The two older vamps were at the computer lab communicating with the high order, apparently through a series of social media ads. The baby vamp was still not sure how that worked. The last thing he wanted to do was get a seminar on the subject from Jerry. Robert and Roldi nearly had to go to ground again before the oldest of the three appeared out of nowhere behind them two nights ago. Jerry's kingdom rested on the shores of Lake Erie, the site of an abandoned amusement park founded by Jerry's father. Opening three years prior to the world-famous Cedar Point thrill park, a subject that is not to be mentioned around the one hundred- and thirty-one-year-old undead man. Some railroad company railroaded the Jenkins family, and the Avon Lake Amusement Land quickly became a desolated three-mile eye sore to the community. In hour two of the explanation, over a feast of fresh bass, it was explained in detail that the Jenkins leased the land to bulk dump companies. This kept anyone from either complaining about the smell or sight of the area and Jerry was left in peace. After his father and mother passed, Jerry, an only child, became obsessed with his only other love, baseball. He built a simple two-bedroom one bathroom rancher, the same simple brick home Roldi and Robert now took refuge, in the center of the large park. Allegedly, Jerry was turned by an artic queen vampire after he hit a triple of off Cy Young while the legendary pitcher was playing a game of pick up before the Spiders spring training. Roldi explained much later that the story was more along the lines of some rogue vamp was crashing at the Jenkins place and took pity on the loner or tried to kill him with a bite to shut him the fuck up and the dweeb survived. After the trio's seafood supper last night, Roldi, with a masked giggle, took off to patrol the outer perimeter. This left Robert with Jerry for hours on end as the two discussed their favorite sport. By the time the subject switched to the Nuns, Robert thought that he now hated baseball. Jerry's knowledge of their enemy was both informative and useful, but the details of the devil hunters were delivered with the enthusiasm of a monotone physics professor. His home was a great hiding spot from the church. Not many holy vigilantes traveled this close to the boarder as they knew there was a peace accord between the Canadians and the vampire order. Something along the lines of vamps helping to protect and breed the endangered animals of the Canadian artic while also keeping their undead eyes peeled for any unwanted Russians. In exchange, the top tier vampires got to live in peace. Freely feast nightly on the overpopulated seals. Robert inquired as to why all vamps do not simply cross the border. The explanation of how cold the region they were expelled to sent frost bitten shivers down his spine. Even to undead skin, the artic winds alone in that region of the north could rip uncovered flesh from bone. Jerry then went on to talk about the Hispanic Nuns, which would have been fascinating as well as terrifying if not for his comatose pitch and overly descriptive narrative. Robert learned that the order of the church that was responsible for eliminating the fang gang, was mostly left to a sacred society of Nuns. Females could slide under the radar of the public much easier. The vast amount of hunters were pulled from church sanctioned orphanages in Central America. The sisters of slaughter, as Jerry named them, were inundated to give their lives to the lord in return from being pulled from poverty. Jerry explained that the two that Robert had run into were just scouts, similar to single-A ball players. Robert was near a comatose state as Jerry went on to describe the more major league hit women. After what really seemed an eternity, Roldi returned with the good news that there was no sign of being tracked. Jerry took his new baseball buddy to a hand-crafted descending room, which oddly sat at the end of the only hallway in the simple house. Upon arrival at the foot of the basement, Robert was to go to the first door on the left, punch in a simple code, then take rest. Jerry manually lowered his new friend to his sleeping quarters. The site of the hidden basement was the first of two fangless jaw dropping moments. Another long hallway greeted Robert once the elevator hit the bottom floor. Much different than the simplistic hardwood flooring upstairs, this hallway had black marble floors that ran at least fifty yards to a sealed black colored steel door. Four other doors sat on each side of the hallway. Robert went to his designated room, punched in the code, and dropped jaw number two ensued. A Victorian era fifteen-hundred-foot luxury suit greeted him. Complete with a king-sized bed, seventy-inch flat screen television, two velvet chaise lounges, and an adjacent roman bathroom with stand-up shower and jacuzzi. Jerry had done some serious renovating over the last century. The cooling shower, which had one of those fancy overhead pressurized systems, felt fantastically refreshing. And the warmth and comfort of the designer sheets and comforter awarded the weeks old vampire his first restful bliss since he became a creature of the night.

Roldi's pounding on the steel front door twelve hours later broke up dreams of chasing blood filled foxes through the forest. The dark lord of night light explained that they quickly needed to check in with the vampire hierarchy to plot their next move. Four hours later, Robert flipped through a thick written account of Carter's brief reign in the oval office.

"Time to roll big Bob," Jerry said. Using his nickname for the former all-star pitcher. Robert started to tell Jerry about his playing days but kept getting interrupted by drawn out tales of old-world recreation softball glory.

"What's the news?" Robert asked.

"The news is no news, which is pretty damn bad news," Jerry responded.

The two headed out of the library and got into Jerry's old pickup. Roldi was nowhere in sight.

"Where's Roldi?" Robert asked.

"Met some chick while he was putting out our feelers," Jerry answered.

"Damn, does he ever give it a rest," Robert exclaimed.

"Hey man, you only live once, well kinda. This one girl I met down in Cincinnati about twenty years ago. She was a librarian. She had really pretty red hair and could do a full split..." Jerry started, and then was cut off by Roldi's sudden appearance which brought great relief to Robert. With all three tucked in the pickup, Jerry took off for home.

"Here is the breakdown. Not a single fucking hint of any response from up north. We lay low tonight, I'm gonna show this book babe my book worm. At early dusk tomorrow we head to Frank's," Roldi explained.

"Slight problem buddy," Jerry said.

"What's that Poindexter?" Roldi asked.

"I got Bob and I game one tickets to the series tomorrow, we are going to have to push the move. And Frank doesn't like me very much," Jerry explained. Robert closed his eyes in response. World Series or not the thought of spending nine innings with the fanged blabbermouth caused an instant headache. Roldi responded.

"One. Frank is gonna have to deal with that shit regardless of what you two idiots got into. Two. Absolutely fucking no way are you two leaving the compound. Those bitches are no doubt setting up shop in and around the city, talking to all the top law dogs. Those saintly sluts will be circling us within forty-eight hours. We head south, lay low, enjoy some mint juleps, and educate old Bobby boy on the rich history of the vampires of the great city of New Orleans," Roldi commanded. The three sat in silence all the way to the entrance of the long dirt road that led to Jerry's humble and not so humble abode. Robert noticed red streaks sliding down the side of Jerry's cheeks. Once in park, the truck sat idle running with the oldest of the three-staring blurry eyed out of the front window. Roldi started again. "What man, what?"

"Well, it's been since forty-eight since the tribe won the big one and since we are on the fly, I won't be able to see any of the games," Jerry explained.

"Bitch, this ain't the eighteen hundreds, you can watch on TV, a laptop, or your damn phone," Roldi said.

"It's not the same, after the heartbreak against the Cubbies, I haven't been right," Jerry pleaded.

Roldi let out a roar and tried to spew reason into the fanatic's temple. "At some point over the next century or two I'm sure that pathetic excuse for a ball club will make it to the big dance again. But you want to risk all of our undead asses to see one game?"

"You think I'm dumb Roldi? How come in all my time, with hundreds of our kind slaughtered, have I managed to go unnoticed? Managed to run the safest and oldest safe house in the region. I know what I'm doing. One game, one night, then we leave the trail stone cold. Please, I beg of you," Jerry pleaded. Only the crashing of small waves from the distance broke up the long silence and then Roldi caved.

"Fine, fine. Fuck me. Bob, you sense anything unusual, you grab his fat ass and head toward Columbus, I will meet up with both of you there. If dumb ass Doubleday refuses to leave, then leave his ass."

"I really think that since I don't know what to actually look for I should really…" Robert started and was quickly cut off by a raised hand from the pissed off dark man.

Jerry flashed a wide toothed smile, wiped the red wetness from his cheeks and the three exited the truck. Robert was about to ask if he could get word to his son since they were moving on and apparently away from imminent danger. He concluded that one was getting a last fuck, one was getting a last game, why should he not get a last wish as well. The fury in which Roldi entered the house quickly derailed that train of thought. Robert thought it wise to maybe wait until they were all in the clear before asking for help in reaching his son.

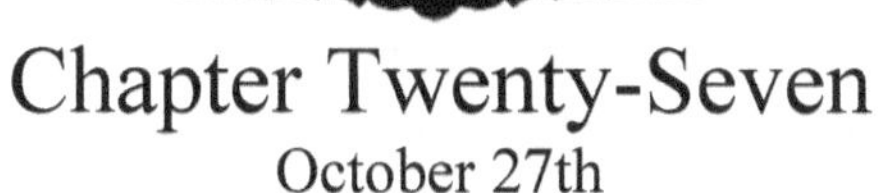

Chapter Twenty-Seven
October 27th

Doctor Robinson greeted his hire, a towering man named Dino, at the front door. The two headed to the back porch, away from the boys and the prying eyes of his sister-in-law. Dino declined a drink before they sat face to face in cushioned wicker chairs. Dino started, "Well boss, I called in every marker I had. There is not much to go on. Which scares the hell out of me. See, when a man like me cannot even get one good damn lead, it can only mean that there are operations at work here that run all the way to the top." Matthew shot out an inquisitive look. This man had come highly recommended. Dino was regularly used by the big pharma companies to pull in information on rivals that threatened their tight knit system. The seedy sleuth was respected and admired for his discretion and ability to unearth the toughest of information gems to find. The good doctor headed over to the deck bar and poured himself a straight bourbon to help dissipate the bad news. Dino started again, "Here is where we are. You don't need me to tell you Sasha was seeing a plastic surgeon, some fat fuck named Timothy Tundrel. From what you told me and hacking into his digital notebook, she went in about five months ago for a consultation and was, with all due respect, pre-paying for her operation. Your father did not go online much, nor did he use his phone regularly, but there is no evidence at all to suggest he knew what was going on there. I know most of the hired men in this region. Not a one of them was called in for any sort of hit that went down at the motel. More scary shit. The department and all of my birdies there have no idea what happened either, except for the bear bullshit story. Even Ronson, the detective that was on the case, is forming his own personal investigation, off the books."

"Was?" Matthew questioned, in between a soft choke from the strength of his drink.

"And here is another thing. He emailed me that he was completely pulled off the case. Not uncommon when someone's partner dies during an investigation. The situation leads to bringing about too much passion, which interferes with reason and all that shit. Thing is, Billy is close to the end of his watch, why he told me to hang tight and keep snooping is beyond me. We all love to avenge a fallen brother, but he and the big man Starkes were not all that close. Now, Starkes looks like he was up to something. Your father was the last man to see some degenerate before his heart gave out. Some guy named Vito Vitalli. Did you know him?" Dino asked.

"Yeah. An old man from the neighborhood. Guy and his kids were all deadbeats. Can't see my father associating with him," Matthew responded.

"Well, your dad, Vito, and two other guys were hanging a bit over the last few weeks. A Tommy Durant and Salvatore Patino. You know these guys?" Dino questioned.

"Yeah, pop hung with them once in a while years ago, but they were no close friends," Matthew explained, as he settled back into the comfy outdoor chair.

"Here's the thing Matthew. There is no damn official report on the motel. And I'm talking about official reports that go to the feds, not the ones filed in court where anyone can catch a glimpse. There is no inquiry into traffic videos the night of the fire. First thing the squad does when something like that goes down is track all the vehicles coming in and out of that area and cross them with highway exit footage. Through my contacts, I have complete access to all of that shit. Well, the two hours of footage from the night of the fire and an hour's worth of timed video from the motel murders have all disappeared. Only time I've ever seen this is when there was a large terror threat in the city about five years ago," Dino explained.

"So, in your professional opinion, what the hell has happened here," Matthew asked.

Dino rubbed his eyes and let out a long sigh. "Two theories on your wife's murder. One. Tundrel had a powerful enemy who came for him and Sasha and the motel manager just happened to be in the wrong place at the wrong time. Two. The degenerate motel manager pissed off some junkie at the place and the junkie took him down, same scenario, Tundrel and Sasha witnessed the incident. Junkie dragged them out into the woods to buy some time. One fact is that either an enemy of Tundrel or the motel manager had to be working with a team. I strongly believe that your father was not involved. The fire and the murders were freak coincidences. No way could one man have pulled off both in that short amount of time. The strength to carry those bodies that deep into the woods three times is uncanny, especially for a seventy-year-old man. As for the fire, well, this man Starkes was a powerful law man. My best guess is that Vitalli was a lot bigger criminal fish than the department suspected. Starkes was lured in there by some big drug lords who torched the place with him in it before the decorated detective busted some covert cartel." Dino explained.

"And what of my father then?" Matthew questioned.

"They have identified all of the bodies and combed the entire area. A very week A.P.B. was put out. That is what is weird. A much stronger outreach should have been called for. The fact that only Ronson came to see you once is also weird. From what you told me on the phone, no other or new teams have come by yet. A shot in the dark, your father is helping the department. Mr. Robinson saw some shit go down with Vito, had some information and is either under their protection from the people behind the fire or helping the law to capture the bastards and get revenge from Starkes. At this point Matthew I can keep digging, but I highly suggest we sit on it for a few weeks. Wait and see if anything comes down the tube from my contacts," Dino answered. Matthew finished his drink with a long gulp and peered over the crystal glass at Dino.

"Crazy. This is all so crazy. One day my father, a moderately wealthy, highly educated man, aged seventy to boot, decides to either become some low-level criminal or has joined with the law to take down some secret society of scumbags," Matthew thought out loud, then burst into a hysterical giggle.

"It is weird, but in my line of work doctor, I've seen weirder," Dino said.

"I'm sure, I'm sure. Thank you Dino, I agree, lets sit on this a bit. I will call you once my father contacts me," Matthew said. Dino tilted his head in reaction to the odd statement. Matthew concluded, "He's alive, I know it. And whatever he has done, or whatever he is doing, My father will contact his son. I fucking know he will."

Robert was loathing the thought of spending an entire evening with Jerry until they walked through the tunnel leading to the left field bleachers. October's darkness had already descended upon the stadium but the bright lights of the ballpark along with the sights and sounds of the pre-game lite up the vampire's undead heart. The chaos and insanity of the last month along with not visiting a live game in years, made the lifelong ballplayer forget about the magic of the game. Sweet smells filled his nocturnal nose. Warm pretzels, freshly steamed hot dogs, perfectly cut grass, the alluring aroma of draft beer, exploded all around the creature of the night. If the former All-American player was suddenly filled with joy, it was nothing compared to the pure ecstasy Jerry was protruding. Fully confident this tribe team would sweep the boys from San Diego, Jerry was a nonstop talking train from the minute they left the compound until they arrived at the stadium. Roldi insisted they drain about an ocean's worth of live fish before they left. Fearing that the euphoria of the event would send Jerry into a feeding frenzy and the sight of thousands of excited fans, exuding blissful blood beneath their flesh hidden veins, would do the same to the baby blood sucker. Robert's blood belly was full, he had no deadly desires as they weaved through the eager crowd in the parking lot. Once inside the stadium, the full throttled vampire was watching batting practice like he never had before. Standing next to his babbling buddy, Robert took in the game with his night eyes. He could just about see the laces on the ball as a monster of a man lined a rope through the infield. A pundit was reading from a teleprompter fifty yards away in the bullpen, Robert could read the words on the small screen clear as day. Jerry sprinted past him to the right after a loud crack of the bat. In slow motion he watched the pudgy man nearly knock over two young boys and leap unnaturally high to bare handedly grasp the batting practice home run. A small applause and some hoots and hollers seeped from the bleachers. The older vampire slapped a few high fives before returning to his seats.

"Did you see that Bob? Barehanded buddy!" Jerry exclaimed.

"Yeah man, thank the lord most of these people are so amped up and buzzed that they only saw a terrific catch and not notice the pudgy guy leap five feet up from a standing position," Robert explained with caution.

"You got to chill dude. I'm gonna get some dogs and beers," Jerry said. Robert nodded as he took in the rest of pre-game with his night eyes.

In 1983 Robert saw the bums in the series. He put it up there with his top ten life experiences of all time. With the exception of meeting Mary and his son's birth, tonight topped the list. He watched his passion like he had never seen it before. The new vampire's entire being just wanted to jump on the field and pitch one inning. From the opening fireworks display until the dramatic final inning, the game and stadium became a living beating entity. Each gladiator on the field moved with the grace of a tiger and executed their plays with the proficiency of a NASA pilot. Robert could sense the players that were nervous, confident, and wired to the max. From the sweat on their brows to the bulging anticipation of their muscles, the players physical anomalies shot raw emotion into his undead eyes. The pensive crowd brought about all forms of emotion. Old men twitching with each pitch, young men screeching with passion in desperation to will the next hit or pitch to glory, and young women filling their passions with desire in response to each game breaking play. In the bottom of the ninth, a three-three pitchers duel, a hero decked in white with grass-stained pants doubled in the game winner as the tribe took game one. Jerry's yelp of joy nearly punctured the ear drums of the couple sitting next to them. Robert closed his eyes, as he let in the delirious roars from the crowd. He concentrated and could hear the vulgar congratulations the hero's team shouted as they all embraced to the left of the pitcher's mound. An hour later the two vampires were finally out of the parking lot as they headed back to the compound.

"Thank you for that. I mean it, that was amazing," Robert spoke softly to his ecstatic friend.

"No sweat dude, I knew you would love it. Wait till you see a hockey game with our eyes. Those boys cuss up a storm during the game. You can hear everything, even from the upper deck," Jerry explained.

"It really is a gift, this thing of ours. I guess it just needs to be controlled, something I'm hoping to learn," Robert said. His eyes shifting out of the side mirror as the horrors of his actions slightly intercepted the glee of the night.

"Dude. You were left out to hang. Katie should never have done what she did. My maker was with me six months before I left the damn house. Every night it gets easier, once we are down south, all of us will show you wonders that you could never imagine. It's really neat," Jerry stated. Robert smiled and enjoyed the simplistic answer from the vampire geek. For the first time since meeting Mr. Blabbermouth, he really started to like Jerry and started to ponder a better new afterlife with this simple man.

"So, do you still think it will be a sweep?" Robert asked.

Jerry eagerly gave his analysis. "I hope so, we were so damn close in 2016, I'm taking nothing for granted. That damn manager leaves our starters in too damn long. If we don't get to them early, it's going to…" SCCCRRREEEACCCCHHHH. The old Ford spun to the right as the brakes were applied with unnatural force. Robert shot forward, cracking his head on the dashboard. He was about to lay into his new buddy when Jerry held his pointer finger to his mouth, signaling silence. Jerry slowly turned to Robert, blood forming at the side of his eyes, and spoke. "They're here."

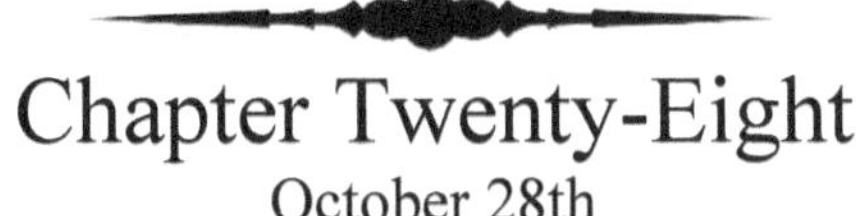

Chapter Twenty-Eight
October 28th

The car clock signaled midnight as Jerry sniffed the cool autumn air like a blood hound.

"Who the fuck is here?" Robert whispered.

"The hunters. I can smell dead human blood," Jerry responded. Robert mimicked his friend and took a whiff through his driver side open window. Nothing, but the older vampire was stronger in his abilities Robert thought.

"Why are we not taking the fuck off then?" Robert whispered again.

"I'll never leave Roldi, he's saved my ass many times. We do not abandon our kind. Get out slowly, then cross over into the brush," Jerry instructed.

Robert quietly opened the creaking door and jogged at pace to the right side of the road. He peered ahead to the dirt entrance of the long driveway that led to the compound. No noise, no scurrying of animals in the brush, no voices crept through the air, just the wicked tune of October's wind pierced the silence. The older vampire snuck around the other side, gazed into the distance, and disappeared toward his home. A minute later he came from behind Robert wearing the mask of despair.

"Fuck me! Don't do that man. I could have taken your head off," Robert clamored, startled by the unexpected deathly silent return of his new buddy.

"They have him. Ten of them," Jerry explained.

"Shit, Ten? We ran into just a couple on the way here and they were bad to the bone," Robert explained.

"Follow me. We are going to attack from the side. I'm going to cut across the front of the house. If I draw at least three of them, you cut behind the house. I will circle around to take out what is left and try to free our boy. Just keep moving, do not try and fight them, you're not strong enough yet. If you do get in a showdown, go for the throat with your hands quickly, then take off again. Here let me get you ready," Jerry explained, he then punched Robert with force on his chin, knocking the newbie flat to the ground. Robert rose fully fanged and clawed, the strike bringing on the change with force. Jerry jogged at human speed as Robert followed.

They came to a clearing about one hundred yards from the front of the house. It took all of his mental fortitude for Robert not to run in the opposite direction. Nine Nuns were standing at eager attention around one very large sister. Jerry whispered something to him about that being Mother Superior. Captain of the crew. She was at least six-foot, dressed head to toe in white while the others were fully drenched in black. All of them with a massive silver cross dangling from their covered necks and all of them held semi-automatic weapons in each hand. What gave Robert the blood-soaked shits was what sat on the porch. A large tanning bed, appearing to be made of pure silver, sat plugged in to one of the outlets in the front of the house. A severed human head rested on top of the elongated electric tanning machine. At closer glance, Robert recoiled as the sweet librarian was parted from her missing lower body.

"Roldi is in that thing. They use it when they capture one of us to get information, it shoots out high UV rays. If you ever find yourself in one of those, just slit your throat," Jerry said.

"How the fuck are we going to get him out of..." Robert started, before being cut off by a loud command, spoken in English with a heavy Spanish accent.

"We know you are here bastards! I can smell your dead breath stinking the lord's air. Come clean and we will send you to the devil quickly. End your suffering!" Mother Superior shouted. A few seconds passed before the large woman hit a button on the side of the machine. Purple beams shot out from the small space that ran along the side of the tanning torture chamber, followed by a horrific howl from Roldi. A lion's purr rose from Jerry.

"On three we go," Jerry mumbled.

"What about the fucking guns?" Robert questioned.

"Zig zag Bob, zig zag," Jerry said, then the old vampire took off into the clearing with the speed of a cheetah.

His roar only interrupted with some insult calling the woman saintly sluts. The sound of bullets ripped through the autumn air like popcorn bursting in a microwave. Jerry miscalculated as nine of the ten went after him with fury and force. Only the big bitch stood idle. Once the front yard was clear, Robert did his part. The baby blood sucker burst from the shrubs shouting. He sprinted toward his captive friend, then darted to the left of the house, toward the abandoned playground. Robert only heard the loud giggle of Mother Superior. After thirty seconds, Robert stood alone in front of a rusted Ferris wheel. More bullets, accompanied with female screams, bounced around the compound. With no clue what to do, and eyes stapled open, Robert crept behind an old Tilt A Whirl. He put his back to the shores of lake Erie and scanned the empty scene. Every few minutes more female shrieks shattered the silence. By his count Jerry was pitching a sinister shut out.

"Back to the brush!" Jerry shouted, coming once again unseen from Robert's left shoulder. Robert began to turn, but his friends gurgling caused him to pause and look back. A silver tipped arrow protruded through Jerry's throat.

"The barn, get to the basement of the baaarrnnn," Jerry sprouted, with blood spewing from his mouth as he took his last words.

A buzzing sound passed Robert's left ear, followed by quick booted footsteps. Two more arrows pierced Jerry. One through his mouth, another through his neck again. The humble old vampire fell face down by the side of his favorite ride. The thud of Jerry hitting the mud sent Robert on the run, he darted back toward the Ferris wheel as Spanish vulgarity followed him in hot pursuit. From the sound of his attacker, there was only one. Robert leapt onto the first carriage of the ride, which sat about five feet off the ground. One silver tipped arrow flew by his right calf another struck his right arm. The death dart tore through the side of his bicep and went clear into the night. His undead flesh sizzled from the silver intake. In response Robert began to leap upwards to each carriage in desperate attempt flee his assailant. Fire shot through the vampire's arm. Putting down her bow, the sister pulled a pistol and misfired shots into the rusted metal. Feeling sheltered in the third carriage, about thirty feet above, Robert dared to peek at the sound below. This crazy bitch was scaling the ride like some spider-woman. Plan in place and sheltered inside the ride, Robert waited for her to reach the cart below. Two more shots pinged off of his swaying hiding spot. Hearing a reload, the injured vampire crawled to the top of the carriage and sprang down on the raven-haired harlot. The sister pointed her pistol at the fanged freak, but the vampire had the jump on her. Robert clattered into her, his weight snapping her knee on impact. She screamed and threw punches with the strength of the lord radiating within her, frail blows to the daunting demon. Robert dug both claws into her temple, twisted as hard as he could and snapped her neck like a twig. After her body went limp, he tossed the Nun like a rag doll against the center poll of the ride, the clang of her skull striking the metal rang a victory bell for the bad guys. Robert jumped from the second cart and landed with unnatural ease on the soft autumn earth. The sound must have been the last death cry from the hit squad, no more roars erupted from Roldi's location. A quick internal debate ensued. Flee and live or fight and probably die, die for good. Flee? Where would he go? How would he get there? With what money? New Orleans? Is that not where they were heading? Didn't Jerry say that city was littered with their kind. North? How far north? How the hell would he even get into Canada. No. He would fight this time. Another friend could not parish. Jerry was dead. Katie was dead. Mary was dead. Human sorrow and anger ended the debate. He would kill this bitch and save his friend at all costs. With the fire of hell in his belly, and an already healing arm, Robert rounded the corner of the house ready to pounce.

"Easy Fangman," Mother Superior spoke. She held a burnt to a crisp, but alive, Roldi, by his dreads with her right hand, her left hand grasped a ninja style samurai silver sword. Robert froze, fangs and claws sprouted ready to end the standoff.

A quick glance at his dark friend sent a brief shiver through his undead spine. Roldi's naked body was covered in bubbling welts, like a million wasp had stung him at once. Only the tiny fluttering of Roldi's eyelids alerted Robert that his friend was still dead alive.

"Hear me out before you both die boy. You are new born. Your fate is not yet determined by the lord. Retract your hideous fangs and talons, take a knee before God, and I leave your friend here to die again another day. You come with me, help us, and your soul might yet be cleansed," The big bitch offered. Robert looked for any kind of signal from his dark friend, nothing came, he fell to the soil, bent his head, and nodded.

In response, Mother Superior forcefully tossed Roldi head first onto the ground and reached behind her stark white top. She pulled a set of shiny handcuffs from a white belt with her right hand, then tossed them in front of the pendulant Robert.

"Put those on slowly Fangman," Mother Superior instructed. Her arrogance accompanying her tone.

Robert grasped the links. Instantly, his fingertips sizzled. Before he could snap on the first painful cuff, several flashes occurred at once, followed by the shrilling shriek of a woman. Roldi turned and sprung at the holy woman, landing one last left-handed swipe across her throat. The highly trained assassin was mortally wounded but got off a sword swipe of her own after taking the blow. Roldi's lower body tumbled like a death deck of cards as his dread head flew from his torso. Long black locks appeared to come to life and scream like medusa's serpents after Perseus's strike. On bended knees and bleeding out, Mother Superior now sat in blood gorged genuflection. Robert waisted not a second. The vampire charged her with the silver cuffs. He lanced the bitch's eyes with the pointed ends, dug deep into her sockets and squeezed until the two ends met deep into her temple.

The first hour after the massacre, Robert just laid flat and stared at the October full moon. Oddly, the sight of the moon encouraged thoughts of werewolves. If vampires existed, did werewolves? And what else? It helped alleviate the horror and solitude of the situation. Hour two, another odd occurrence ensued. Being the Catholic boy that he was. Robert gathered up his two very dead friends and dug separate graves for both, no cross to mark the graves for two reasons. One. He had no idea what or if any religion both Jerry and Roldi worshiped, and he did not want to disrespect them. Two. Once the next set of sisters arrived, he did not want his friends remains desecrated. After covering the deep ditch with filthy and blood-soaked clawed hands, Robert went into the house. He poured a glassful of merlot from the box wine in the fridge. Jerry was a class act through and through. He tilted the now decapitated Mother Superior's head over the glass to let a few drops fall in. Robert rested on the plaid couch and contemplated his escape. The barn. Jerry said something about a barn. There were seven small barns all around the property. The exhausted vampire finished his victory toast, took an ice shower, then covered himself in some of Jerry's sports sweats. Two hours later, arriving at barn six, the crack of dawn sprouted fear in Robert. He would go to ground if nothing sprang up at this location. If the inevitable next hit squad found him so be it. The night life had drained his undead soul. Only the necessity to get word to his son kept him going. Like the previous six shacks, nothing appeared to take form of some secret until he noticed a bulge under an old red wagon. On his knees, Robert saw a black latch, he tossed the wagon to the side and pulled the trap door open. A narrow wooden ladder led to a dusty floor. With nocturnal vision he saw a switch to his right. He flicked it up with his middle finger. The light exposed a narrowing hall that led to a wider birth. Robert climbed down the ladder, then pulled the door shut, it was more exposed with the wagon gone, but could buy him some time if they came back. Forty feet later there was another switch. After flicking this one, beams of white florescent revealed what looked like a massive bank vault, with a twisting seal handle protruding from the steel wall. Robert approached and sent up a silent prayer that there was no secret code to get in. He turned the handle left to right and barely budged it. Using vampiric force on the next take, the handle budged, then twisted like a loose wheel until a pop sound burst from the dusted edges. Robert grabbed the exposed edge and softly opened the entrance. His unfanged mouth dropped at the sight before him. A massive bed sat about thirty yards in the distance. In front of the bed was a large flat screen and a medium sized refrigerator rested to the left of the mounted TV. A steel ladder sat at the corner of the room that led to another handled vault style hatch above, clearly an exit hole. But what was most shocking was the amount of sealed money wrapped and encompassing the walls leading to the bed. All hundred dollar bills neatly wrapped and stacked. Robert figured at least a couple hundred thousand in cash acting as expensive wall paper. Jerry carved out a nice panic room, cozy, secure, and littered with cash. Robert closed the opening; another hissing sound signaled the lock setting. The war weary undead warrior sat idle on the side of the massive bed. Staring at and past the large flat screen, Robert's eyes began to expand back to human settings and swell with red liquid. There was enough money in the room to help him lay low for years, but none of it could bring back Jerry, Roldi, Katie, or Mary. Thoughts of Mary brought forth a cavalcade of undead crimson tears. Robert tossed his frame backwards onto the extravagant bed. He glanced at the simple ceiling under wet eyes. Time got lost in reflection and before exhaustion gave way to sleep, the vampire knew what he had to do to set it all right.

Chapter Twenty-Nine
October 29th

Bishop Lopez strode into the great hall with arrogance in abundance. He knew he handled the situation well locally. He was not concerned from the night's report.

"All has been silenced your eminence," the Bishop pronounced. He bowed to the seated Cardinal, kissing the holy man's large ruby ring. Turning to his assistant, the Bishop grasped a large manilla envelope and humbly placed it in the hands of his spiritual superior as one might hand their sins to the lord above.

The Cardinal opened the document and examined the forms and photos. Snapshots of Ronson's framed suicide were scattered amongst the alleged freak shooting of Dino Salaris. The Cardinal began a brief inquisition,

"The head lawman, Mueller. How has he reacted."

"He is on board. At first, he asked that his detective be given time to let all pass. But after I told him the man would go to Starkes's home and then call around, Mueller got the drift of things to come. The department will wash their hands of this mess. Many cops take their own lives when their duty is done. The ghost of that hard life haunt them until their last breath. I read the man Ronson well, a tragedy yes, but he was skilled. It would only be a matter of time before he put it all together. We are so close to extinction level. No stone must be left to litter the sands of his sanctity," the Bishop explained.

"He sits with the lord now. His great sacrifice will grant him a seat at the holy table. We shall pray and give praise to his name. Mister William Blyth Ronson," The Cardinal declared. Everyone in the room bowed their heads for a moment, then the Cardinal questioned the other loose end.

"And Salaris. What news from the vile streets?"

"That one was a little easier. The man carried a stained soul. Pervert and turncoat. The fee the doctor paid him was the only reason he attacked the case with such vigor. Something along the lines of a six-figure reward for the return of his father. Salaris was getting close, even had an elusive gypsy lined up. The one who consistently dodges us with far too much ease. But we will bring her to the light soon enough," the Bishop explained.

"And the doctor. Robinson?" The Cardinal questioned.

"Great news, he rehired already. The man loved his father. The woman leading his case now serves us. She will steer him clear of the dark truth and put closure to the poor man's suffering with an official death certificate and ashes to boot," the Bishop exclaimed with glee.

"Loved? Do you not mean loves? Reports are we have a squad dead and still no trace of this foul fiend," The Cardinal said, anger and fury rising with each syllable.

"Our lone wolf has scoured the location in Ohio. Two down one to go. The wolf will slaughter the scared sheep. We have every reason to believe from an intercepted email that he will head south to that unholy city," the Bishop said.

"I fear he will head north to be protected by the winds of eternal winter and that vile government. Perhaps you should oversee the rest of this mess and put an end to it," The Cardinal instructed.

"As you command your eminence," the Bishop humbly replied.

"I have not seen Bobby since the fire hun," Sal explained.

"Damn, I like really, really, really need to talk to him," Luna said.

"It's been all batshit since the fire. No one knows what happened to him. My boy says that word from some local cops is that he is a major suspect. They even think he killed Vito," Sal said.

"Bobby? No way man. He had a heart of gold. Bobby was such a gentleman. I don't think he could have hurt a fly." Luna said.

"Look at Ted Bundy. Everyone thought he was the bee's knees. Turned out the guy was a friggin maniac. It's always the quiet ones," Sal lectured.

"Well shit. If ya hear something give me a ring would ya? And thanks for seeing me. I know they are getting strict on visitors right now," Luna said. Sal took the sticky pad with her number on it. A little heart was drawn under the number. He moved to the edge of his bed with a smirk and plumped his fat ass down.

"I gotta ask. And I don't mean any disrespect. But how much Vito pay your girls to hang with us and you know?" Sal asked. Luna turned and giggled, "Why big boy, how much you got?"

"I can do a hundie for a short shift. How's that sound moon child?" Sal questioned.

Luna turned toward the mirror that sat on top of Sal's dresser. She slowly took off her top. Sal backwards crawled to the head of his bed and started to lower his jogging pants. After removing her bra, Luna admired herself in the mirror. The extra twenty pounds she had carried the last five years gave way to a fit new V-shaped tummy. She gave herself a full fanged smile, then turned closed lipped to her temporary employer.

"Sounds great big boy. No need to apologize either. Hey, a girl's gotta eat."

"You got to give it a rest babe," Kyle said. He strolled over to his lover and pecked him on the top of his head. Bruce responded, "I will, I will, I promise. Go ahead to bed, I'll be there in a few." He would go to bed in a few. A few hours. For the last several days the young man became obsessed with all things vampire. Kyle's eyes told no lies when he explained his attack. Debbie was a fool, but an honest fool. Both of their undead tales too similar to be ignored. Bruce tried to contact his old co-worker. He wanted to apologize, he wanted to tell him how he and Kyle were doing great and had formed a life plan. But, most of all he wanted to see if the myth was true, and if so, he really wanted a quick nip from his old pal.

Chapter Thirty
October 30th

In game two, the Tribe won in a waltz. Robert hoped there was some afterlife for his new race, so that Jerry would be enjoying what looked like an inevitable series win for his boys. Jerry, who ended up being so damn rich and so damn clever in the end. That insanely boring uninteresting man had not only built an amazing high end panic room but also set up covert monitors all over his grounds, which feed a live stream through the flat screen. When Robert awoke from his slumber, he first went to the fridge to enjoy a cool blood cocktail, one of about fifty Jerry had prepared for a dark doomsday. Next, the vampire scoped the live feed. Robert noticed a diminutive man decked in roseries and sporting a thick white beard singe last night scenes. The odd man sniffed and scoped the grounds for hours with the concentration and determination of a champion prize fighter. Even with his obvious skill, the small man missed Robert's barn hideout and one other small shack that sat near the edge of the large lake. After his scouting trip, the bearded man piled all of the Nuns and the headless henchwoman in a pile, then sent their ashes to the lord. Not only shockingly clever, but Jerry must also have been a great warrior as well. From the site of the bloody bonfire, slaughtered sisters were torn limb from limb, their stunned final faces gave fact that they were hit without warning. After torching the women, the odd man genuflected and stayed knelt for over three hours. Impressive, even if the vampire knew that man would take his head in a split second, or worse, put him in one of those scary sun beds. Robert scanned the monitors once more before setting out. The man and his old Cadillac were gone. If the bearded stalker appeared, Robert had a dead sprint exit strategy in place. Once he lifted the ceiling vault, he knew there would be no need for an immediate escape. No scent of any human or threat lingered in the all hallows eve air. Robert knew what he was looking for inside the house, eventually finding it in one of the kitchen drawers. The somber vampire sat at Jerry's simple dining room table and penned a goodbye. He removed one of the envelopes from another drawer. Robert returned to the living room to glance over the final words he would ever say to his beloved son. Tiny, soft, red dots speckled the common piece of paper. Robert took a deep breath and red out loud.

"My dearest son Matthew,
 My boy. I cannot imagine the pain and suffering you must be going through right now. I must write quick to explain, as this will be my last night on the planet. Do not ever weep for your father. I lived a thousand lives during my time. I cherished each second with you and your mother. I will digress with the specifics because you will think I've got mad. By unusual circumstances son, I turned into something. Well. Something beyond reason. I became a monster in more ways than one. Whatever the police or anyone else tells you, please know this. I killed Sasha. Please know it was in a blind rage and not premediated. I only wanted to expose her untrue nature to you as her indiscretions came to my attention. I know, I just know in my heart that you will move on and find love again. Please son, try to find love again. As well, I am responsible for the fire at the apartments and once again under no ration or reason did I kill anyone by purposeful intent. What time and circumstance have made me is of no fault of mine, just a freak accident. As a man I hope you once loved, please forgive my vile actions. I apologize for any shame I may have brought upon you. You have all of my accounts. I suggest you drain them quickly as the law and the church may seize my life's savings. Please do not send anyone to look for me. Your father is dead. Only a shadow of my former self remains and that shadow will be cast into eternal darkness by the time you get this letter. Do not trust any law enforcement nor anyone coming to you under the veil of Jesus himself. I must go now. Please share stories of the man you loved with the boys and not the man who I unknowingly became. I plea for you to forget the last few weeks and move on to a happy and prosperous life. Being your father was the greatest privilege of my life. Live well son.
 Pop."

Chapter Thirty-One
October 31st

The small seaside town was quite as a tomb. Robert strolled down main street during the first hour of Halloween. World Series posters, pennants, and flags waived with force from the early winter wind. Robert located a post box. Fighting back the onset of more crimson tears, he sent off his last words to his son. No time to weep, he had business to finish. A quick sprint past the last few shops on the strip, where glares from windows covered with mummies, three eyed purple aliens and fellow fang toothed figures, all wished him a fond farewell. Quickly, Robert reached the run-down boat yard. Growing up around the Chesapeake, he was educated as to where to find what he needed. Grateful that most of the boats were dry docked and that nobody appeared to be around. Not even a night guard, which signaled the quaint seaside village was a lot more trusting and secure than his home town. Prepared to hot wire any watercraft, his night eyes spotted a small runabout. His only concern was if the small boat would be able to carry the heavy load he had lifted earlier. A few moments later he kicked the small engine over. Robert was pleased when the small craft did not start to tip forward from the weight. Eager to complete his mission, the undead man and his cargo missed a dark buoy by inches which would have shot his plan straight to shit. A few drops from the historic lake hit his face. The icy water felt frigid, even to his undead skin. The focused vampire almost turned around. He contemplated coming up with a new plan, but what was done was done and Robert needed this all to end. He cut the engine about a full mile from shore and glanced back at the world he knew. His undead eyes could still make out the dim lights from the small dock bar from where he departed. Thoughts of hundreds of nights at bayside bars that he and Mary had spent drinking flavored rum, and laughing the night away, brought an odd calm over him. It was a good life. No dammit, it was a great life. He had no control over what had happened. Robert decided all of this during his long ponder inside of Jerry's self-captive steel cell. He got to live. He got to live well, and dammit he was a rare creature that got to die well. Before anymore thoughts could cloud his judgement, Robert went to work. The strong vampire fastened the thick steel around his waist, then slug more chain around his feet. Finally, he attached a heavy stone to the end of the steel links. The moment he felt the strength of the footed noose, Robert tilted over the side of the small craft and hit the freezing water with little splash. At first, the icy water burned his vampiric skin, but after the initial shock, his undead body adjusted to the temperatures. Bass and other sea life darted away from the unusual, but frightening creature, as he sunk to the sandy bottom quickly. Once the large stone hit the base of the lake, Robert gave a tug. He was worried that he had the power to lift back to the surface if reason and fear changed his mind. At second attempt at lunging forward, he knew he did his job well. Knowing he would probably not drown due to having no breath, the thought of eternally floating at the bottom of the lake sent a shrill through him, but he wanted a self-imposed prison. As predicted, five minutes later, there were no signs that he would die of drowning. Robert had no breath to draw short of, no beating heart to erupt out of fear, and no body temperature that would cause a deadly hypothermic reaction. As planned, he would just be.

About the Author

Lance W. Reedinger is a horror author residing in Baltimore, Maryland. He is the author of Claws and Goblins. His short story Prancer was featured in the 2021 anthology The Colour Out Of Deathleham. Lance is the senior contributor at horror-nation.com.

www.ingramcontent.com/pod-product-compliance
Lightning Source LLC
Chambersburg PA
CBHW021157110726
47900CB00002B/614